MW00957057

Breaking the Fog

Breaking the Fog

The Essence Chronicles – Book One

C. C. Mitchell

First printing: 2019

ISBN 9781795293945

C. C. Mitchell

PO Box 248

Comptche, CA 95427

www.ccmitchellwriting.wordpress.com

For my family—

Who inspire me every day and
who always believed I could do it.

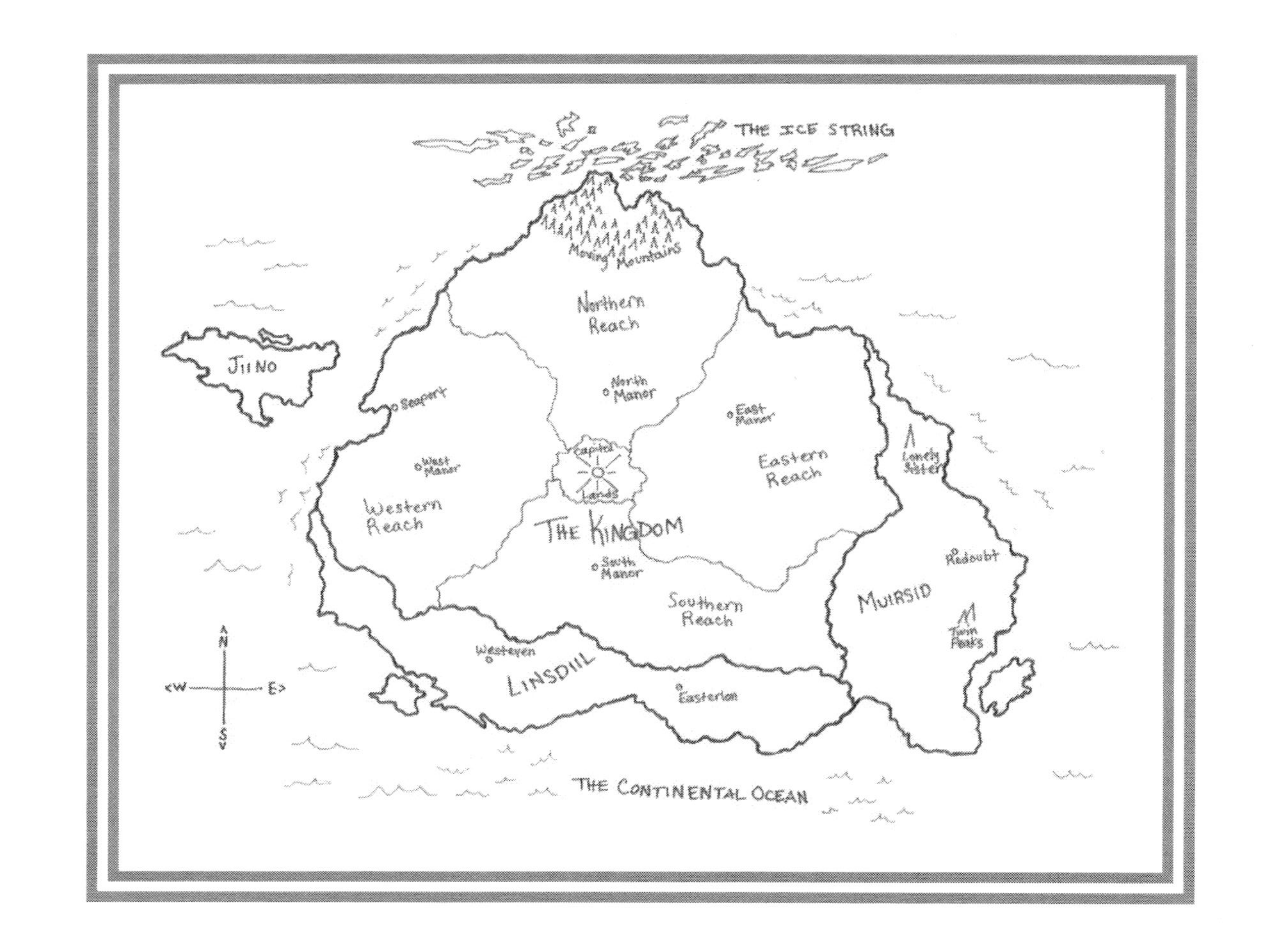

THE ICE STRING
Moving Mountains
Northern Reach
North Manor
Jiino
Seaport
West Manor
Western Reach
Capitol
Lands
East Manor
Eastern Reach
THE KINGDOM
South Manor
Southern Reach
Lonely Sister
Redoubt
MUIRSID
Twin Peaks
N
W
E
S
Westeyen
LINSDIIL
Easterlan
THE CONTINENTAL OCEAN

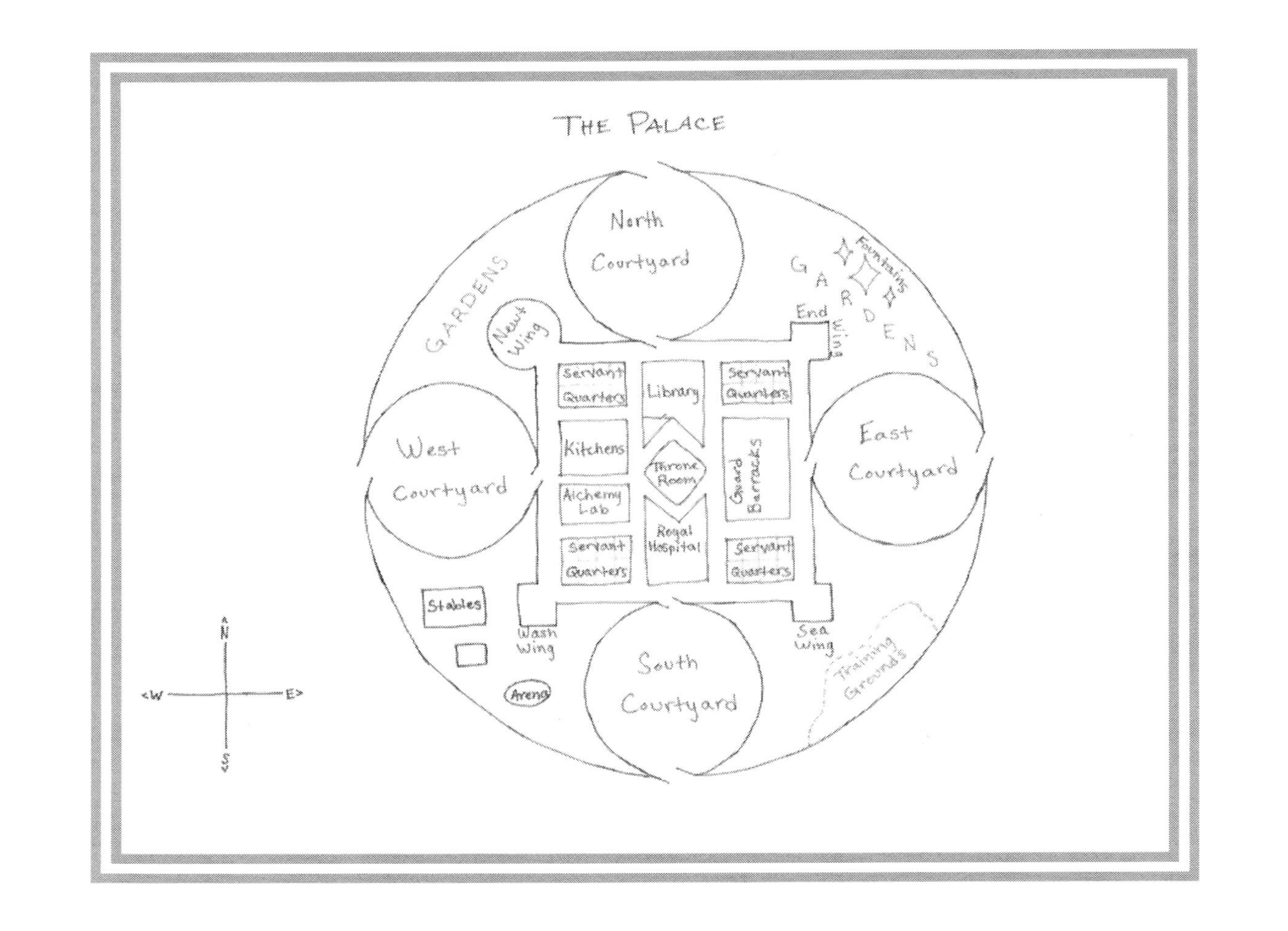
THE PALACE
North Courtyard
GARDENS
Fountains
GARDENS
New Wing
End Wing
Servant Quarters
Library
Servant Quarters
West Courtyard
Kitchens
Throne Room
Guard Barracks
East Courtyard
Alchemy Lab
Regal Hospital
Servant Quarters
Servant Quarters
Stables
Wash Wing
Sea Wing
Training Grounds
South Courtyard
Arena
N
<W
E>
S

1
Wander

THE WORLD TURNED RED as the sun glanced across my face. Gentle heat bloomed along my cheek, the crimson light burning through my eyelids. I rolled my head to the side and drew my brows tight. The heat and its glow subsided, the warmth escaping my skin into cool shadow.

Sounds of a forest crept into my ears, sneaking past the hum and whine in my head that gradually gave way as I listened. Birds chattered and trilled, their songs accompanied by the rustle and scrape of leaves. A rough, hard surface pressed into my cheek and stabbed against my temple. I opened my eyes and was greeted by the gnarled, cracked surface of a thick root. Just inches from the tip of my nose the root disappeared into lush green moss.

I lifted my head, blinking long and slow to clear the haze of sleep that clouded my vision. Rays of pale sun cascaded in pillars through the branches of the trees to speckle the forest floor. I rose up on one elbow, pressing my back against the twisted bark of the tree that had guarded me through the dark, moonless hours.

A shuddering breath rattled my lungs as fear flared to life in my veins. He might still be out there, slipping like a phantom between the dark trunks hunting me, watching and waiting. Tremors shook my arms and legs. He would never stop searching.

I remembered pain and blood, my blood spilled on dresses and nightgowns; the creak and groan of a stubborn old door opening on weathered hinges. I remembered someone helping me, someone I cared for, and then all I knew was the night sky. Wind had seared my cheeks and slashed through my hair as I fled, the muscles of my body shrieking from under use and the sudden strain. When I had tumbled to the ground under the cover of the forest, exhaustion had enveloped me like the silken wings of bats, and I dreamed of the eyes of predators glowing in the darkness.

I dug through my mind, tugging at memories farther and farther back in time. My father's face flashed across my vision. It was the look he had worn on the day he sold me, cold and indifferent. My memories surrounding that day were fragmented and jumbled. I couldn't piece them back together any more than I could push through the cloud that shrouded everything that followed.

My instincts told me to run as far and as fast as I could, but where was I going? I pressed my back against the tree, pushing into the sharp ridges of its bark until they gouged the skin of my shoulders through the tattered fabric of my dress. I breathed deeply through my nose and let it out again through my mouth.

My mind was a snarled mess of lost thoughts and impulsive instincts. My heart pounded in my ears and my lungs felt tight. If my pursuer was nearby, they would have already captured me, but I had to keep moving. It didn't matter where I went, I just had to move.

I focused on the strong wood at my back and my own steady breathing. I slowly slid up the trunk of the tree, tiny pieces of dark brown bark chipping away and scattering around my feet. Ignoring the stiffness in my muscles, I squared my shoulders and took a few steps forward. A sharp tug on my dress brought me to a halt. There was a jagged tear in my skirt that left a strip of soiled fabric dragging on the ground, which was trapped beneath the thin sole of my sandal. I tore it away and dropped it onto the moss, lifting my skirts and starting forward again.

I stepped carefully over the thick roots that protruded from the forest floor. I looked at the tall, straight trees and imagined that they were the only reason the world did not crumble under its own wretchedness.

My gait was slow and halting as I navigated around low branches and spindly saplings growing at odd angles. Every snapped twig, chirp of a bird, chatter of a squirrel, or grunt of a deer stopped me in my tracks. My eyes darted from one shadow to the next, the back of my neck prickling. The sun rose before me throughout the morning and I clung to the sight of it like I hadn't been able to cling to my father a year before. It would be a long time before I was sure of myself, but never again would I be drug away like an animal to slaughter.

The light of the morning hours shimmered and danced along the surface of the leaves and flowed between the branches of the trees. Light coated the moss-covered ground in brilliance and the roots that broke the surface seemed to pulse with a similar luster.

I watched as the sunlight lost its gentle playfulness when morning shifted to midday. It became stern and sure, guiding my feet forward to an unknown destination. The steadiness of the beams gave me strength as I wandered and hoped for a place where I could be safe again.

By the time the sun was behind me and fading over the edge of the world my legs and feet ached, sharp pangs shooting through my bones and muscles. I refused to stop until I could no longer see between the trees. I found a soft patch of moss under some woody brush that bent into a small shelter. Lying on my back, I inched underneath it sideways, careful to avoid the stiff, spidery branches.

Curled beneath my shelter, I watched the sliver of a moon rise in fragments through the forest canopy. Pieces of it would disappear and reappear every few minutes. It held my gaze until my sight blurred, and I fell into the dark of the surrounding night.

Fabric stretched across the space above me and cascaded down smooth wooden poles to a rug-covered floor. The stone walls were adorned with colorful weavings and beautiful landscape paintings. To the left was a heavy, dark wood door that had etchings of vines and small birds across its surface. A woman shoved it open and came bustling into the room.

"Hurry my dear! You must sit up at least!" she whispered urgently, pulling me into a sitting position. Sharp stabs of pain jolted up my spine and into my shoulders, causing me to whimper. "I know, dear, but we must, or it will only be worse!"

At that moment the door opened again, and a man glided into the room, his dark robes swirling around him as if carried by a wind. He was tall with light brown hair and striking golden eyes. Panic rose up the back of my throat and my eyes darted about the room, looking for some way to escape.

"Good morning, my joy!" he exclaimed, taking my hands in his and kissing my forehead lightly. "Bena, you may leave us now," he ordered the woman.

"Yes, my Lord," she replied, curtsying and fleeing the room with a worried glance. My stomach clenched as I watched her go.

"Now, what do you say we have some fun, eh?" he asked me quietly, his eyes sparkling.

He coaxed me off the bed and led me toward the large double windows opposite the door. He dropped my hands and opened the windows, revealing a covered courtyard with tall trees clustered around a green pond. He drew me toward the edge and a soft wind lifted the ends of my tangled hair.

"You know what to do," he said, smiling expectantly at me.

I gave him a blank stare, wondering what he could possibly mean.

"Has the drink made you foolish, girl?" he exclaimed, all joy vanishing from his face. As he spoke, his teeth grew long and pointed, and his fingernails stretched into black claws. His yellow eyes glowed, flashing in anger as he slashed one hand across my back.

The blow brought me to my knees and a moment later small, golden feathers began to appear on my arms and across my body underneath the torn nightgown. Heat and pressure built along my spine and then burst outward across the backs of my shoulders. A scream tore from my lips and a moment later feathered golden wings drooped along my sides, tinged brown by dried and fresh blood.

"Get up," the man ordered, still looking feral, like a wild cat.

I stood slowly, keeping my gaze on the floor. My legs trembled beneath the thin shift I wore.

"Good, now fly." He gestured toward the courtyard.

I didn't move.

"I said, fly!" he snarled, lifting his hand again.

I screeched and jumped out the window frantically. The wings caught me, and I desperately clung to the nearest tree, my entire body quivering. My nightgown fluttered to the ground below, like a white flag.

The man laughed from where he stood in the window. My wings ached and flight made the tearing pain in my shoulders worse. I clenched my teeth and labored to the next tree, and then to the next. I jerked through the air, trying to get as far away from his horrid laughter as I could. The glass walls and ceiling twinkled in the autumn sunlight like the glint off of sharp teeth.

2
Strange

I SAT UP ABRUPTLY, scratching my forehead on the spindly branches above. The sun hadn't risen over the horizon, but I knew I would not get any more sleep that night. Emerging from my mossy bed, the dream nagged at my thoughts. It had felt far too real and sent chills coursing through my body.

The birds began to sing to each other, and squirrels added their chatter to the ambiance of the forest as I wandered between the trees. By the time the first rays of sunlight peeked over the edge of the world, I had reached a small brook that faintly babbled across its bed of rocks. The water seemed to cheerily encourage me to follow its trickling sounds.

I tiptoed along its moss-covered banks through the forest. The air became more humid the farther I walked, and the brook gradually turned into a creek and then a stream as wide as I am tall. Judging by the sun, following the stream had turned me south.

The stream widened a foot or two more and then I heard tumbling and splashing that became louder and louder. The trees began to recede from the edge of the water so that I walked underneath open sky. When the sun was at its highest, and the heat drug at my legs and beat down on my head and shoulders, I found the waterfall that was the source of the rumble. It was not the largest of waterfalls, but it was large enough to leave a round pool underneath its tumbling waters.

I scrambled down the damp slope at the edge of the falls, slipping and sliding down to the rocky shore that rimmed the pool. The faint sting and ache of bruises tickled along my arms and down to my legs. I stepped onto the bank of the pool and realized that I had felt no external pain during my trek through the forest. The fatigue of my muscles and creaking of my bones made their protests all too clearly. There were other wounds and bruises all over my body that I did not feel.

I searched the bank and found a rock with a sharp edge. I pressed it to the back of my arm and scraped until a few drops of blood emerged on the surface of my skin. I felt nothing but the pressure of the rock on my arm. My skin was numb.

I threw the rock into the water and began to tear at myself in a panic. I kicked off my tattered sandals and tore the sleeves off of my woolen outer dress. I untied the sash around my waist and yanked the heavy fabric over my head, tossing it into a cluster of boulders near the falls. I tore and pulled and screamed silently until all I had on were my undergarments. The thin gown of white fabric was identical to the one I had worn in the dream.

The realization filled me with rage. I began to tear at the slight garment as well, but then I noticed the bruises and scratches that covered my feet and legs. I looked to my arms and they were just as discolored. I groaned in anguish as I realized how much physical sensation I was not feeling. I became afraid that I may never feel again, and the fear drowned out my anger for a few moments.

I sat heavily on the shore, my head in my hands and elbows resting on my knees. I was too afraid to cry, though I desperately wanted to sob and scream. Somehow, I just couldn't. Maybe my tears had all been spent and there were none left to fall.

After allowing my thoughts to drift for a long time, I made myself stop thinking about what more *he* may have done to me. I stood and slowly walked to where I had thrown my gown. It was tossed between a few boulders that sat between the shore of the pool and the forest. I placed my thin chemise on top of the wool dress and went to the edge of the water. I waded to the center of the pool and floated on my back taking long, slow deep breaths.

The underwater sound of the falls was like a lullaby and the movement of the gentle waves rocked my worries away. Warm sunlight caressed my cheeks as I closed my eyes and gladly drifted into sleep.

The air was cool, and the small pond rested calmly at my feet. Its emerald waters reflected the dome that arched above the tiny grove. I sat on the wooden bench at the edge of the pond, surrounded by proud, straight trees that would have grown much taller had they not been confined.

There was the faint click *of a door opening on the other side of the courtyard. I sat up abruptly, my instincts causing anticipation and fear. The door closed and there was no sound of footsteps, which I had expected, but my mind still became more alert with every second that passed.*

"There you are. I've been looking for you." His voice purred from behind me, much closer than I had anticipated.

My eyes widened and my shoulders tensed.

"How long have you been out here, my love?" he asked softly, silently coming into view and sitting beside me on the bench.

I could not answer because I did not know. He did not like it when I didn't answer, but if I did, then he would think I was lying, and he liked it even less when I lied. I stared at the green pool before us.

He leaned forward so he could see my face better and gently placed his hand atop mine, which rested limply in my lap. I flinched at his touch but did not dare pull away, though it seemed he was in a reasonable mood for once.

The emptiness in my face must have concerned him because he slid from the bench and crouched before me on the ground. His face was then level with mine, though I did not want to meet his eyes. He had never knelt or sat on the ground in my presence. The fact that he was frightened me.

"Will you not look at me?" he said, sounding rather desperate. I knew that I should, but I could not control my body or my mind.

He stood and softly coaxed my body to stand with him. He guided me to the edge of the grove where we stood before the huge windows that opened into the grove from my bedroom. I gazed up at them blankly, barely remembering what they were. He touched my shoulder lightly, causing me to tip my head in his direction. After I vaguely acknowledged his presence at my side, he carefully slipped his arms under me and lifted my feet off the ground. When I showed no sign of panic or even recognition at his motions, he bent his knees and jumped effortlessly from the courtyard to the edge of the window. He proceeded across the room and gently placed me on the bed.

"I shall return soon, my joy," he whispered, brushing his lips across my forehead. He left the room, easily pulling open the thick door to the corridor outside.

I didn't bother to try and keep track of how long he was gone. I was enthralled by the texture and color of the canopy that hung lazily above the bed. I barely noticed when he came back in, with the little woman close behind.

"My Lord, you said to never give her fresh water," she said, looking very confused.

"I know I did, Bena!" he snapped. "She has had nothing but the drink for too long. It is making her mind duller than I had intended."

He sat on the edge of the bed and managed to turn a sparse amount of my attention toward him. Enough that he could help me to drink the cool water that he had returned with in a clay mug.

"We will have to find a reasonable balance between the drink and fresh water, or she will wither away into a mindless husk," he growled.

3
Steps

MY FEET SCRAMBLED on the bottom of the pool as I tried to sit up. My head slipped under and water filled my mouth. I stood, planting my feet in the loose bottom as my heart raced and I gulped in air. I looked up at the sun and the sky spun. I jerked my eyes back down to steady myself and watched as the water of the pool gently lapped against my shoulder.

My body was suddenly fatally thirsty; I lifted a handful to my mouth, and then another, and another, until my stomach lurched sluggishly. Bile rose up the back of my throat, my body telling me to stop.

I laid back on the water again, this time sensing the sunlight and the water in a different way and the sensations that filled my mind and body were, for once, an indulgence instead of an escape.

Just a little while later the sun slid into late afternoon and the air distinctly dropped in temperature. My mouth began to feel dry and my tongue was like sandpaper. I paid no attention to it at first, and then my throat began to burn.

I desperately wanted to drink all the water around me to make the feeling go away but knew it wouldn't help. I stood up and waded toward the edge of the pool, sucking in as much air as I could to appease the burn. I stumbled onto the shore and fumbled for my clothes, attempting to put them back on my wet body with stiff fingers.

Once I had my shabby sandals back on, I shuffled toward the trees that ringed the waterfall. I collapsed against a tree and slid to the ground. My muscles went limp and I swallowed repeatedly, but the burn continued to rage in my throat. It spread into my arms and down into my stomach, seeming to follow the flow of blood through my body. It took all my will and strength to lift a trembling hand to my face, scraping drenched golden hair from my cheek.

As I sat gasping, nearly paralyzed, I heard the repeated soft *thump* of what I thought were hooves on moss. The steps became louder until two men on horseback emerged from the trees to my left. They moved to the edge of the water and allowed their mounts to drink while surveying the surrounding scenery. They weren't very old, but they weren't young either; at the most they could have been twice my age, which would put them in their mid-thirties.

The boulders sat between the men and me and the shadows from the trees fell over me like dark silk. All the same, the man that stood along the curved edge of the pool, gave an expression of surprise when his scanning gaze swept over where I sat. He said something to his companion, who turned in the saddle perched on his dark gray horse's back and stared intently in my direction. A few moments later they steered their horses around the cluster of boulders and toward the trees.

My breathing came in ragged gasps as pressure began to build along my spine and I desperately struggled to push it back down. I refused to be overpowered by the panic brought on by imminent capture.

"Well, would you look at that! Seems like a young maiden lost in the forest," remarked the man who had seen me first, sliding off his horse. The other man did the same. They continued toward me cautiously, hands in front of them, as though they were afraid I would run off.

Both men were of average height and build, nothing too imposing or slight, and both had sun-streaked brown hair, though the second man's hair was lighter. The first man had a mischievous glint in his gray eyes that would have been appealing if the situation were different. The second man was more grizzled and rugged in appearance with sad, mud colored eyes that said he had fought for every moment of his life.

They came within an arms distance and darted for my arms and legs. I weakly batted them away a couple times before my limbs failed me and I was hauled to my feet. They tried to drag me to the horses, but my knees gave out as soon as they pulled in any direction.

The one with sad eyes scooped me up off the ground and easily carried me to one of the horses. His companion swung up onto the chestnut animal and I was placed in front of him. I leaned heavily against his chest and my head fell onto one of his shoulders, my heart beating frantically. I prayed that they would not take me back to *him*; anywhere but the place I had run away from.

"Looks like we won't have to go hunting for another prize after all," my supporter commented, making the other one laugh as we set off into the forest.

We rode for what seemed like forever because of my state of internal agony. Just before the sun set, we broke through the forest onto a narrow road. I hoped that since it was getting dark, we would stop for the night, but my captors had different plans.

The moon rose slowly, illuminating the trees and the road in pale silver while the shadows around them grew thicker. Yellow eyes flickered in those shadows as the burning in my blood flared. The searing in my veins and the silent screams that filled my head brought those shadows and their hungry eyes crowding in until they were all I could see.

There were bars on the tiny square window that was set crookedly in the little door to my right. The man sitting across from me on the other cushioned bench jerked the velvet curtain over the window as soon as he saw me looking at it.

"Where are you taking me?" I asked, glaring at him.

"To a place where your life will be more comfortable," he answered, obviously bored even though we had been in the carriage for less than an hour. "Don't worry; I'm sure you'll like it." He stifled a yawn.

"If I'm going to like it so much, why didn't my father tell me I was going to live somewhere else? Why did he sell me, and why must I be shackled?" I demanded, lifting my arms straight out in front of me, rattling the chains that hung from my wrists to emphasize my point.

"Please try to be a little quieter. I can't stand loud noises," he requested, lazily pressing his fingertips to his temples. How could someone who was so uninterested in everything possibly stay so skinny?

Just as I was about to rebuke his avoidance of my questions with some incredibly unattractive insult, the carriage went over a washboard of bumps and I lost my retort.

4
Traders

"ARE YOU CRAZY?!" someone exclaimed much too close to my ear. "She's too pretty to sell to Slavers! Don't you know what they'd do to her?"

The lingering effects of sleep retreated, and I fought the tension threatening to roll through my muscles at the reference to Slavers. They were dirty men who loved dirty money and filthy transactions. If I were sold to Slavers, they would put me in shackles and chain me to one of their creaking wagons. They would turn me into their personal whore and when my health declined far enough, they would sell me as a scullery maid to some rich man in Muirsid for a ridiculously high price who would also do whatever he pleased with me.

"Well, what do you propose then? That's what we've always done in the past, unless you've taken a liking to her already?"

I opened my eyes just enough to see that it was light out and then shut them again.

"I have not! I would just rather take her to Tuscal, since he has a reputation of finding better homes and still pays a fair price," the first man answered.

I relaxed a little, realizing they were Traders. Traders used goods and medicine or trinkets as their currency most of the time. If they did take me to this Tuscal, then they would trade me for a healthy amount of food, some jewels or medicines that they could take and sell legally in any town or city; whatever Tuscal did with me after that was his business.

"The last time I saw him he tried to take my head off!"

I still sat corkscrewed sideways on my captor's lap as we jolted forward with every step the horse took. There was a crick in my neck and my shoulders ached. The sound of the horses' hooves was much sharper and clearer than before so we must have reached a cobblestone road instead of the dirt roads that ran close to the forest.

"That's because the last time you saw him you were trying to steal the gold out of his store in the middle of the night!" the man I rode with replied. His companion must have had an amusing expression because he started laughing and then both of them were silent for a while.

"Look, there's the capital. We're well on our way to Tuscal's shop," the first man teased his sour friend as we came to the top of a hill. I had never seen the capital and I could not pretend to sleep any longer, so I opened my eyes and gawked at the expanse of the city.

It was not all towers and stone like I had imagined, though the houses on the very edge of the city, outside the wall, were made of gray stone and most had thatched roofs. The majority of the buildings inside the capital were either sandstone or painted wood with brightly colored tile roofs. The buildings gradually got bigger towards the center of the city where the palace accentuated the splendor of the capital. The city was surrounded by acres upon acres of farmland and orchards full of fruit trees; in one area I thought I may have even spotted a vineyard.

I could not see the palace as clearly as I would have liked, but what I could see was the domed glass that capped every tower and the central structure of the palace. As a child I had heard stories about the grand palace that so few had the privilege to see. No one from our village had ever been near the capital and we were always eager to hear tales about it from passing merchants and vendors.

The cobblestone road grew wider as we traveled through the fields, coming ever closer to the wall. There was a line of people and animals and carts going into the city. The commotion was something I had never heard before. The people were yelling or talking and the animals grunted, squawked, or neighed over the sound of wheels creaking and rumbling. As we joined the long procession, I thought I might go mad from all the things I had never seen or heard before.

"Would you look at that? The sleeping beauty finally awakens!"

I looked up at the man who carried me. He laughed at the overwhelmed look on my face.

"I guess you've never been to a city before?" he asked.

I shook my head in response.

"Well, a word of advice to you then: Try not to take it all in at once. Instead, focus on one thing and then another until it all gets more familiar."

"Yeah, and I wonder what you really mean by 'familiar'," the other man remarked out the corner of his mouth.

"Don't mind him. He isn't always this bitter; it's just the lack of sleep on a long ride," my transporter assured me. "I'm Ned and old sourpuss over there is Kurt."

"Since when do we give our names to captives?" Kurt demanded.

"You mean, since when do *I* give *your* name to captives?" Ned jested, causing Kurt to grumble in his saddle.

By the time we came close enough to see the carvings on the outside of the gate's archway it had been a full day since I had sat by the waterfall. The archway was decorated with simple and elegant floral vine designs that wound their way to the top of the arch where they encircled a brilliant sun.

"See Kurt, it's always a good idea to ride through the night when we can. If we hadn't it would've been a whole day later before we got here," Ned pointed out smugly.

"Yeah, yeah, gloat all you want. I'm just glad I'll soon be snoozing away in a nice feather bed at the Rosehip Inn."

While they bantered back and forth, I tested my body. The paralyzing effect from the day before seemed to be gone, but my bottom was sore from riding between Ned and the horn of his saddle. If I shifted either leg just slightly, I could feel the peppering of bruises that I had seen the day before. I wanted to revel in the return of sensation in my body, but my arms and legs were still stiff and tender from the reaction to the water.

There were two guards posted on either side of the gate, watching people as they filed in and out of the city. When we came close enough to one of the pairs to attract their attention, they moved forward and stopped us in front of the arch. We were the only travelers that had two seated on a horse or even had more than one horse. As I looked around, I realized the people around us all had carts with or without oxen and only a few had a horse or a shabby pony.

"What business do you have in the capital today?" one of them asked, obviously suspicious.

"We have come to see an herbalist about a remedy for berries that have a strange effect on a person," Kurt replied.

"Who is this?" the guard gestured towards me.

"She is our sister. She ate the berries we speak of and hasn't been able to say a word since. We told her not to, but she's always been a little crooked in the head," Ned told him.

I wanted to pinch him for his remark about being daft but decided to play the part and just sat staring blankly ahead.

Out of the corner of my eye I could see the sword strapped to the left side of his saddle and I could sense the tension in the left side of his body as he prepared to arm himself. If I spoke up, it would cause a scene, and someone would come to harm. The guards would also want to know where I had come from and those were questions that I did not want to answer.

"Hmm… Very well, carry on," the guards dismissed us, moving back to their post. We rode past, the shadow of the archway hiding the afternoon sun for a moment until we reached the other side of the gates.

"It wasn't caused by berries, but guards don't know anything about herbs," Ned murmured quietly, his head bent over my ear slightly. I shrugged stiffly in response, not understanding what he meant or knowing what to say.

The road continued on straight through the city. I could see in the distance where it ended at the vertical bars of the gate to the palace. Both sides of the road were lined with the stands of merchants, trinket sellers, and fruit vendors. No wonder the front gate was so busy; the market was just inside its doors.

There were so many people and carts that it seemed like our horses were wading through a sea of color. Every stand, carriage, cart, and person were a different color. If the fabric roof of one stand was purple, the next might be orange or blue and it was the same with the carts and carriages. Each person wore a different color and their skin was all different colors as well. I had seen white people and brown people, but I had never seen people that looked like the night or a red sunset.

I gaped at everything around me and was disappointed when we turned off the main street into an alley that led to another, slightly quieter street. We wound our way through the city mostly by alleyways and obscure paths between shops and houses. We turned so many times that I lost count.

We stopped at the back door of a shop that seemed to be on the other side of the city even though I could still see the domes of the palace. We had gone in a crooked arc across a quarter of the city while never getting any closer or farther away from the palace.

The shop was sandstone with a blue tile roof and red doors. Kurt dismounted and knocked on the door. A moment later it was opened by a middle-aged woman with red-tinted skin who looked as though she'd had a hard life.

"Yes, what do you want?" she said sharply, her eyes narrowing.

"We have business with Tuscal," Kurt replied, no friendlier than she had been. She looked him up and down, then saw Ned and I out of the corner of her eye. I tried not to fidget, still perched between Ned's arms on the horse, as she studied us carefully.

"Wait here," she ordered after a long, tense moment. She slammed the door in Kurt's face then her voice rang inside the shop.

Kurt came back over to the horses and motioned for Ned to let me down. He shifted and carefully placed me in Kurt's grasp where he set me on my feet next to the horse. While Ned dismounted, Kurt kept a firm grasp on my arm, a little too firm. Ned tied the horses to a rail to the right of the door and then took up position on my other side while we waited for the woman to come back.

The door was pulled open roughly. The woman stood to the side of it, a short hallway stretching out behind her. Halfway up the hall stairs took off to the left. Two closed doors stood on the right side of the hallway.

"Come on, he's waiting for you." The woman waved us in impatiently.

Kurt stepped through the door first. Ned nudged me forward and the woman shoved it closed after he stepped through behind me. We paused in the hallway while she clicked locks into place and then sidled around us. She crooked a finger and we followed her up the stairs to another hallway. There was a large alcove directly across from the top of the stairway with shelves full of exotic jewelry, small jars, and dried plants.

The woman turned left again, and I looked behind us as we followed her. A red door stood at the far end of the hall, to the right of the stairs, the muffled sounds of a busy shopfront leaking around its hinges.

We were led into a small study with blank walls and a desk that seemed too large for the room. The man that sat behind the desk was equally as large. His face was nearly hidden behind a full beard and graying dark curly hair that sat in a thick helmet above his forehead.

"What have you brought me today, Daon?" he asked the woman cheerfully as she crossed the room to stand beside him.

"Traders," she replied simply.

"Ah, my favorite business acquaintances!" He looked up from the papers he was carefully sorting through. "I didn't fancy seeing you ever again, Kurt." His expression darkened a little, but his attention was quickly diverted as he fixed his gaze on me. "What's your story my dear?"

"She hasn't made a sound since we found her. We think she got into some Miasma Root," Ned spoke for me.

"Why do you believe that?"

"We found her nearly unconscious next to a waterfall and her eyes had a brown glaze to them. It's still there, faintly," Ned explained, gesturing toward my face.

"Is that so?" the man raised his eyebrows and stood, shifting around the desk to look down at me.

I was afraid he might break through the ceiling he was so tall. He stared intently into my face, studying my eyes.

"Well, look at that... You were right, and right to bring her to me," he said softly. The strange expression on his face made my spine tingle. A moment later it was gone, and he turned toward the woman saying, "Daon, would you show her to a room while I negotiate with these gentlemen?"

I didn't know what any of them were talking about, but I had a feeling that I might be able to get some answers.

"Yes, sir," she grunted, crossing the room and gently taking my arm.

She turned me toward the door and led me back down the hall to the stairs. Our footsteps echoed in the hollow space below the wooden staircase. At the bottom of the stairs, she showed me to a door on the left.

She opened the door and said, "Anything you might need should be inside, but if there's anything else come see me. I'll be in the storeroom." Then she went back up the stairs, leaving me to myself.

I looked down the hall, towards the door through which we had entered the shop. I went to the edge of the stairs and listened for a little while to see if there was anyone nearby. There were muffled voices but nothing close, so I slipped down the hall to the door. It had three sets of locks on it, not including the one in the handle: one padlock, a chain, and a metal bar that slid from one side of the door frame to the other. All of the external locks were obviously engaged and when I turned the handle it was locked as well. There was no chance I could get out that way.

My curiosity partially satisfied, I returned to the open door that led to the small room on the other side of the stairs. The room was sparsely furnished with a small wooden table and two chairs on one side of the room and a cot with a small colorfully patched quilt on the other. There were no windows and the walls were bare sandstone like the rest of the building.

There were some cooler clothes and a sack of food on the table. Folded neatly was a long, cream-colored cotton tunic to replace my wool dress and underneath the tunic was a pair of lighter sandals than the ones I wore. The sack contained a small loaf of bread and a wedge of cheese along with a bright red apple, which I was surprised to see because any kind of fruit, aside from the wild berries that I had grown up on, was a luxury.

I exchanged my ruined dress for the cotton tunic and sat heavily on a chair. I ate part of the bread and most of the cheese and then began to nibble on the apple. The first bite burst in my mouth, the juice coating my tongue with a sweetness that I savored and a slight sourness that reminded me I was still in the real world.

As I crunched softly on the delectable fruit, I began to wonder about the place in which I sat. What kind of shop was it exactly? The man that was in charge seemed decent enough, but could he be trusted? And what about the woman, Daon, could I trust her? The answer would be no until a later point in time; I had made a grave mistake by trusting too easily in the past.

"The sun has set. Tuscal will meet with you in the morning. Get some rest," the woman said from the doorway, startling me out of my thoughts. I gave her a slight nod in acknowledgement, and she disappeared around the edge of the door frame.

I finished the apple, disappointed that it was gone so soon, and glanced at the cot. I was exhausted and yearned for sleep, but I also wondered what memory I might dream about once I closed my eyes.

Everything glowed with soft yellow light. As my vision cleared, the high-ceilinged hall decorated with paintings, rugs, elaborately carved and cushioned chairs and couches came into focus. Gold embossed vines wove up the walls, around the huge windows, and across the vaulted ceiling. I sat in one of the chairs next to a tall door on the left side of the room.

The sun was incredibly bright outside and I turned away from the burning light. The crack between the door and its frame caught my eye. I closed one eye and peered through the crack from where I sat. The skinny man from the carriage was speaking to another man. I strained to hear what they were saying.

"...during the journey?"

"My ears still ache, my Lord. Constant questions the whole ride, no matter how I tried to deter her. She is not someone I would choose to house," the skinny man said, clearly agitated.

"Very interesting... But you are not the one who will house her," the other man replied.

"Yes, but—"

"Quiet! I have already completed the deal with her father. She stays! You are dismissed."

"Yes, my Lord." The skinny man looked at his shoes, bowed slightly,

and turned to leave the room.

"Tenley," the man called, making him turn back, "would you ask Bena to make something for breakfast?"

"Yes, my Lord," he replied. A door on the other side of the room clicked shut. Footsteps came toward me and I turned to face the light-filled spacious hall.

"Miss Fobess?" a smooth voice said from the doorway. I looked up, straight into eyes like twin suns. I blinked, refocusing as he shut the door behind him.

"Yes?" I stood and turned to face him.

I had never seen anyone like him. He was much taller than anyone I had ever known with a strong boned face and fiery eyes.

"I am very pleased you came. Allow me to introduce myself. I am Lord Sars Rafas, overseer of the Northern and Eastern Reaches of the Kingdom, which includes your village to the west," he said smoothly, bowing deeply with a flourish of his arm. As he bowed, I saw that his tawny brown hair was tied loosely at the base of his neck with a thin strip of leather.

"A pleasure, I'm sure," I replied shortly, curtsying just barely. "Why am I here and why did you buy me?" I glared up at him, daring him to lie.

"Tenley certainly was correct," he laughed softly to himself. "I made a deal with your father because he needed money and you are precisely what I require."

"Require? According to my father, all I'm good for is dropping water buckets and never arriving on time. Why in the world would anybody want me?" I crossed my arms.

"The reason I need you is because the Kingdom requires the Lords

and Ladies of the Reaches to take in one unfortunate soul every year. It is part of our duties to the Kingdom to train people so that they can better their own lives and use their skills to serve the Kingdom and its citizens."

"I still don't understand," I grumbled.

"Boys might become soldiers and girls could become a lady's personal servant in exchange for comfortable housing and plenty of good food," he explained with a smile. There was a suspicious glint in his eye that made me uneasy when he added, "In short, you are here to train."

5
Different

I WOKE FEELING TENSE and uncertain. There were odd rattling noises and the sound of chairs scraping and doors opening and closing coming from above. Someone ran down the stairs and opened the door to the room next to mine, knocked something over and then ran back upstairs after slamming the door shut again.

As I opened my eyes and looked around the room, I was surprised that I easily remembered everything that had happened since the waterfall. I still had no recollection of anything prior to that. It seemed as though all my thoughts and memories simply vanished into a fog that drifted lazily through my mind.

I listened to the peculiar noises in the building around me as I sat up and shoved the quilt aside. I stood and slowly went to the table where the sack of food and my old dress still lay. I had just sat down and began to eat the rest of the bread when there were heavy footfalls coming down the stairs with a softer, almost impossibly quiet set of footsteps close behind. A moment later, loud knocking rattled my door.

"Come in," I called, my voice still thick from sleep. The door opened instantly and the large man from the day before filled the room as he walked toward the table.

"Good morn to you, my dear," he exclaimed. "Do you feel any better than you did before?" He sat heavily in the other chair and gazed at me from across the table.

"Yes, I do, thank you," I replied. Daon slipped into the room quietly and took up her position lurking behind the man.

"Wonderful! Nothing a good night's sleep and some fruit won't cure, eh? Isn't that true?" he addressed both Daon and I. We both nodded slightly. "Well, in any case, I might as well introduce myself. I am Malvin Tuscal, merchant of the finer foreign herbs and trinkets, at your service!" He stood and nearly swept the floor with his bow, causing me to have the strangest desire to giggle.

"I am very pleased to meet you Master Tuscal," I replied, inclining my head in acknowledgement. "I am Nika Fobess."

"Ahh… Nika… A wonderful name; strong and victorious," he said, grinning as he lowered himself back into the chair. "And please, just call me Malvin."

"My name hasn't brought me much luck in the past," I murmured, mostly to myself.

"You are strong though. From what I understand, anyone who had that much Miasma toxin in their system should be dead," he argued.

"What is Miasma toxin?"

"It comes from the roots of the Miasma plant. Nasty stuff. Makes you forget everything you know and learn if you have enough of it. A small amount just makes a person light-headed for a day," Malvin explained. "That's how it got the name Miasma; it means cloud or fog."

"That would definitely explain a lot of things," I said, half to myself. Now I knew why I only remembered the past year in pockets of time. "How is it that the water I drank in the forest remedied the toxin though? It was just water."

"That is a curious truth indeed. No one knows exactly how, but fresh water that hasn't been mixed with anything else simply neutralizes the toxin and cures the symptoms."

"Sir, shouldn't we be discussing other matters?" Daon spoke up from where she stood in the shadows by the doorway.

"Ah, yes, of course! You always manage to steer me back on track, Daon." Malvin grinned over his shoulder at her. "I suppose it is time to get down to business."

"I assume this business includes me." I rubbed my palms lightly on the cotton fabric of the tunic covering my thighs.

"You are correct. Although, to be exact, *this* business *is* you. I am very glad Kurt and Ned chose to bring you to me instead of any other Trader, and especially any Slaver," he began.

I gazed at him, waiting for further explanation.

"Have you heard anything about me at all?" Malvin asked.

"I'm afraid I have not," I replied earnestly.

"Well, aside from fine foreign herbs and trinkets, I specialize in removing fine people from the more tragic of situations; mostly those found by Traders and the awful Slavers that are not permitted to enter the city. Sometimes I will employ one of the more noble Traders to take some unfortunate souls off the Slavers' hands when those rascals have the audacity to come close enough to the capital.

"So, today I will visit my good friends around the city, in the company of Daon, and find a household that may be in need of another lady's maid or kitchen hand. Just to be clear, I do not sell living beings; I am in essence a Trader much like those who brought you here, although I like to think of myself as a little more sophisticated in my business. I trade for services and favors that allow me to keep both my occupations running smoothly," he explained, taking a deep breath and pausing for a moment. "You do know how to act as a maid?"

"Yes, I do. I have had some training," I responded, nodding.

"Wonderful! I will go up to my study, put a few things in order, and then be off. While I finish some things, Daon will introduce you to our other resident and she, in turn, will show you how to run the shop in case I don't find another place for you quickly or you have to come back at any time," he said, standing and taking a single step to the door. He paused and added, winking, "Be sure not to get into too much more trouble while we're out." His steps echoed through the building as he climbed the stairs.

"If you are ready, come with me please," Daon said.

I stood, following her out of the little room and up the stairs to the storeroom. From there we turned right, toward a door that had a window of orange-tinged bubbled glass set in the top half. All I could see of what was on the other side were shadows and movement.

The door opened into an area separated from the rest of the shop by a three-sided counter. The center of the counter was bare while the sides were covered with glittering jewelry and precious stones and metals that were all obviously foreign. The only metal and precious stones that I had ever seen were brought out of the mine back in my home town, and they were copper or iron and dark emeralds. All these pieces of jewelry were finely crafted out of gold or silver and rubies, sapphires, or occasionally amber.

Tables were scattered around the room that also held strange and wonderful objects. The walls were blanketed with dried plants that I had never seen before and the tables that were nearest the walls sported tiny jars filled with powders and sticky-looking liquids of all different colors.

"Eith, this is our newest resident," Daon said to someone as the door swung shut, drawing my attention away from the interior of the shop.

There was a girl perhaps a couple years older than me standing by an inconspicuous cubby in the underside of the front counter. She was small and thin with a soft face and a pointed chin; her hair was as dark as night and fell over porcelain skin into deep blue eyes.

"Oh, it's wonderful to meet you! I wanted to see you yesterday but, by the time I finished up in the shop, it was too late," she exclaimed cheerfully, coming forward to squeeze my hands with a giant smile spread across her gentle features. "I'm Eith Liffei, a fellow rescue of Malvin's."

"I'm Nika Fobess," I replied, squeezing her hands in return. "It is lovely to meet you as well."

"While Malvin and I are out, Eith will teach you how to run the store and anything else that pertains to the tasks. I wish you a good day," Daon said. She dipped her head and slipped back through the door.

"Daon is nice enough, but so serious! I still don't know how to act around her," Eith said, sounding wistful. "Anyway, back to the tasks at hand, correct?" She was smiling again and dropped my hands to sort through the cubby underneath the counter. When she turned around, she was holding a string of silver and gold coins. "Do you know how to count money?"

"Yes, I believe I do," I replied, bobbing my head.

"Wonderful! The last girl Malvin rescued couldn't even form a single letter on a page. Luckily one of the local Ladies needed another washerwoman and I didn't have to explain *everything* to her for very long," she said, returning the strands to their hiding place. "Come with me and I will show you where everything is and tell you about the other tasks we need to do besides count money." She motioned for me to follow her as she lifted the center of the counter and ducked through the opening.

"We don't have to know what everything is, but we do have to know the general areas where things should be," she explained. "Herbs are on the walls and minerals are placed on the tables nearest the walls as well as plant-derived tonics and ointments. The tables in the center of the room hold samples of our gold, silver, bronze, and gemstone jewelry. Everything we sell comes from outside the Kingdom, but don't be surprised if some dolt asks if something is made in house or somewhere else in the city."

After gesturing to everything in turn, Eith led me back through the counter and then into the storeroom at the top of the stairs.

"As I'm sure you already know, this is the storeroom. Herbs are on the top shelves, jewelry in the middle, and minerals and ointments are on the bottom," she pointed out. "Most of the shelves are labeled, which makes restocking easier, and that," Eith said, gesturing towards an old long handled broom in a corner, "is our most trusted utensil."

"Are there very many utensils?" I asked.

"Just jars and boxes really, but out of all of them the broom is a shop keep's best friend," she explained, spinning on her toes and holding the orange-windowed door open for me. I moved past her back into the front of the store and she closed the door behind us. "That's the end of the tour, and now it is opening time!"

Eith danced around the corner and across the shop floor to another, solid wood door. She twisted a series of locks and then pulled the door open with obvious effort as it scraped across the floor. Pale sunlight flooded the opening, spilling across the plank floor and the nearest tables, causing the contents of the shop to sparkle like it housed hundreds of tiny stars.

"Eith, don't you ever worry about robbers? Everything here looks so valuable," I wondered, taking in the magnificent sight.

"The streets are well protected by Kingdom soldiers," she replied, the expression on her face indicating that she understood my concern. "They keep a handle on anything that might happen and are very vigilant. Plus, Malvin has his own protections in place, just through reputation and connections with the crown. Almost no one is stupid enough or desperate enough to try and steal anything from here."

I nodded my comprehension as our first customer walked through the door.

Within the first few hours of business, I felt like we had served half the city. There wasn't even five minutes where there weren't customers in the shop. Eith and I divided the duties, so I took money for the items and she ran from one end of the room to the other and into the storeroom, providing what the customers asked for. By the time noon came around, both of us were on the verge of collapsing. The customers that were currently in the store finished their business and Eith locked the shop door behind them when they left.

"All stores in the city that do not serve food close at lunch so employees can have reasonable resting time. It prevents the owners from overworking those that are employed. Not that Malvin would do that anyway," she explained when I gave her an inquisitive look.

"Well, do we have any food?" I replied. "I'm starving."

"Of course, Daon and I keep a special cupboard full in the back.

Malvin has his own stash in his office," she said.

She led me back into the storeroom to a white cupboard that I had not seen earlier, right over the broom's resting place. There were three shelves inside; the bottom shelf was filled with fruit and some vegetables, the middle shelf held loaves of bread, rolls, and pastries, while the top shelf was full of small, brown clay jugs of water and various juices.

Eith handed me a red apple that was so shiny I could almost see my reflection on its surface, a large roll that I later found out was filled with a myriad of spices, and she pulled down a jug along with two small clay cups. She chose the same items for herself and sat down in the middle of the storeroom floor after closing the cupboard. I joined her and we ate in silence for a while until all that was left was the unopened jug. Eith uncorked it and poured a purple liquid into the two cups.

"What is it?" I asked, taking the cup she slid toward me.

"Grape juice," she answered, taking a large swallow and sighing contentedly. "It's my favorite; I think it's the most refreshing."

I took a cautious sip of the strange substance and practically fell over backward from the explosion of flavor. It was the richest thing I had ever tasted and had a mustiness that was also sweet and sour all at once. As soon as I swallowed, I almost immediately felt like I could take care of a city's worth of customers in one hour.

"I see what you mean," I said breathily, downing the rest of the juice. Eith laughed and poured each of us another cupful.

"How did you end up under Malvin Tuscal's humble protection anyway?" she asked politely.

"That's what I would like to know," I sighed, putting my empty cup down.

"You don't know?"

"All I know is that two men brought me here because they thought I was too pretty to go to Slavers, and they found me in the forest next to a waterfall. I can't remember anything that happened before I ended up in the forest, aside from pain and suffering," I explained. "That and Malvin said I was drugged when I came here."

"Well, that is certainly more interesting than my own story," she grumbled.

"What is your story, Eith?"

"Well, years ago, when I was still a girl, my family oversaw the Eastern Reach of the Kingdom, but, when my father died, our Reach was merged with the Northern Reach, by suggestion of Lord Rafas, of course. Thus, our noble status was lowered, and we were forced to move to the capital," she stood and took the jug back to the cupboard and stacked the cups on the top of the cupboard.

"On our journey here, my mother and I were taken by Slavers. My older brother, who had left a year earlier, is one of the High Prince's personal guards and tried everything he could to find us, but Slavers are very good at erasing true trails and creating ones that never existed. My mother, who was not a very strong person, died after a month of traveling. When the Slavers reached their post by the capital, Malvin took me off their hands and here I am," she concluded, raising her arms above her head.

"How do you know your brother was trying to find you?" I asked, taking a deep breath and working through the shock of hearing Lord Rafas's name. I flexed my fingers, trying to alleviate the prickling sensation under my fingernails.

"I saw him and other soldiers from the back of a wagon, questioning some of the Slavers, but we were being taken through the trees on a secret path, bound and gagged."

"Do you really think my story is more interesting than yours? I don't think it is."

"I've lived mine, yours is a mystery; so yes, yours is much more interesting," she said, beaming.

I shook my head and stood up as she started to open the orange-windowed door. I followed her through and shut the door behind me, taking my place behind the counter as Eith reopened the shop.

Hours later, after watching the sun's rays streak through the open door and slide across the shop floor, Eith and I saw the last customer out the door. Before we could close the front door, someone had to sweep all the mud and grime tracked in by innumerable boots across the floor and down the steps, which was my job since I didn't know how to restock or where the shop's wares needed to be placed.

I froze mid swing when I got to the steps, the broom forgotten in my hands. Everything in the street was bursting with color and life, despite the time of day. It wasn't nearly as crowded as the main street into the capital and all the buildings were clearly businesses, each just as unique as the one next to it.

There were many different kinds of silk shops, a simple store with delicate slippers in the display window, and one that seemed to sell paints and brushes. The best view, though, was to my left. Down at the end of the street the domes of the palace were mesmerizing as they sparkled in the sunset, making the crystal look like pale gold.

"Beautiful isn't it?" Eith said, startling me. She had walked up beside me on the threshold silently. She was also gazing at the palace. "Sometimes the royal family comes up this street to buy silks from those shops across from us. Once, when the princes came, I saw my brother." She lowered her face and I could see the pain clearly in the stature of her tiny frame.

"Did you go speak to him?" I asked, watching her.

"No, I was too afraid. I don't know why," she replied, ashamed.

"Oh, Eith... Come on, let's finish up and see if Malvin and Daon are back yet." I wrapped an arm around her shoulders and led her back inside. I helped her start restocking the storefront again and then I returned to sweeping. I looked across the stone street and could only imagine the sensations Eith must have experienced upon realizing her brother was less than fifty feet away.

"They're back!" Eith shouted from inside just as I finished the last step. I bounded up the steps and Eith scraped the door shut behind me, latching all the various locks. We went to the top of the stairs by the storeroom just as Daon and Malvin were coming up.

"Good eve, my dears! How did the shop fair today?" Malvin asked. His grin was weary and didn't quite reach his eyes. He removed the large floppy hat he was wearing and handed it to Daon then started unclasping his cloak.

"It was as busy as usual, but so much better with a second person," Eith told him proudly.

"That is wonderful! How was it for you, Nika?"

"I have never experienced anything in the city before, so I'm still trying to take it all in. How was your other business?"

"Not so well," Malvin muttered, heading to his office down the hall, leaving the three of us at the top of the stairs.

"He's disappointed," Daon said simply and followed him down the hall. I looked at Eith and she shrugged in response, starting down the stairs.

"Maybe tomorrow I can show you around the neighborhood if Malvin and Daon stay here," she suggested gaily, glancing back at me as we descended. "Sometimes after lunch Malvin takes over and I can go explore, providing, of course, that I'm careful."

"I would like that very much. I've never seen a city before." I beamed as we reached the bottom.

"Sounds like a plan," she smiled back, "but for right now, I will see you in the morning." She gave me a hug and then disappeared inside her room.

I did the same, practically falling onto the bed. My legs and feet burned with exhaustion, but thoughts of Eith's situation kept flitting through my mind. I wished I could help her but didn't know how.

The carriage rattled and jolted, catapulting me across the foot space. I squealed as I flew through the air and came down with a thunk, *accidentally landing with my elbow in his stomach. He groaned and doubled over as I scrambled back to my seat.*

"I am so sorry, my Lord! Are you all right?" I exclaimed, reaching out toward him.

"No, no, I'm fine. Accidents happen," he assured me, waving my hand away.

I let it drop back into my lap, joining my other on the rich dark green velvet of the dress he had given me the day before for our journey. It was midwinter and he thought I needed a better gown for the cold, and that none of the dresses that had come with me from home suited me at all.

Just then I looked out the window, a gate and wall coming into view. The wall was of large gray stones and the gate was made of thick wood planks. The braces of the giant hinges were wrought in the image of branches that stretched across the face of the gate. As we approached, one side of the gate opened and we entered a round courtyard, much like the one at the other grounds, where I had first become acquainted with Lord Rafas.

The carriage slowed to a stop and the door to my right was opened, revealing Tenley and his icy politeness that thoroughly irked me.

"I trust the road wasn't too troublesome, my Lord?" he asked, pointedly glancing at me while bowing respectfully as Lord Rafas exited the carriage.

"It was perfectly fine, thank you, Tenley," Lord Rafas replied, dismissing his butler's behavior.

He turned to take my hand as I stepped down. The carriage pulled away and he led me up the steps toward the front doors of the gigantic house.

"Welcome to East Manor, my dear," he said, enthusiastically.

"It's very lovely, but how is it that you live in two manors?" I asked. He gave a short laugh and opened the door, gesturing for me to enter.

"The previous owners could no longer perform the duties required by the Kingdom, so this Reach was merged with mine. I can oversee the East just as well from North Manor, but every other month I come stay here just for good measure," he explained. "So, as long as you stay with me, this will

be your new home as well."

A smile took over his features that I couldn't quite place. I blinked at him, thinking I wasn't seeing clearly. For some reason his teeth appeared more pointed than usual.

6
Experiences

I WOKE WITH A START as someone shook me awake. I bolted upright to discover it was only Eith.

"What in the name of the Kingdom are you doing?" I asked her breathlessly.

"You were moaning and groaning and wouldn't wake up when I knocked on the door, so I had to do something. The shop is opening in a few minutes. I don't know where Malvin and Daon are and we should have been up there already," she explained, gesticulating wildly toward the second floor of the shop.

"Alright, alright, I'm up now!" I exclaimed, throwing the blanket off and scrambling out of the small bed.

We jogged up the stairs to the storefront and I prepared the counter while Eith checked all the tables and then heaved the thick door open, on the other side of which there were already two customers. She apologized for the late opening and expressed that there had been a complication in the back that had needed to be taken care of. I smiled to myself as she told her only half-fictional story.

Our day began, and remained, equally as hectic as the day before, if not more so. By the time lunch came around, I was almost ready to drop to the floor. I do not know how Eith fared but standing behind the counter for hours counting money and maintaining a pleasant smile really made my feet scream. Just as before, we closed the shop for lunch, consumed our midday meal and then Eith practically skipped off to Malvin's office, leaving me on the floor of the storeroom with the remainder of our lunch.

I placed the leftover food back in its rightful places and the used dishes on top of the cupboard. The door to Malvin's office opened and a moment later Eith grabbed my arm. She pulled me along with her as she marched toward the front of the shop.

"Malvin said he has a meeting right after opening, but once he is finished, we can go out." Her eyes glistened with excitement.

"Where will we be going?" I asked. She left me behind the counter and pirouetted around the room before going to the front door.

"Oh, around, I suppose. It's the city! We don't have to plan where we're going, as long as we don't get lost," she replied, heaving the door open once more.

Malvin's appointment arrived shortly afterwards and Eith instructed me to pull a beaded string that hung from the ceiling in a corner behind the counter. A moment later Daon appeared through the orange-windowed door and said she would show the man to Malvin's office.

Eith and I spun in circles tending to customers for what seemed to be another whole hour before there was a break in business and we could sit on the floor behind the counter. For the first few minutes we leaned against the wall almost entirely limp, until Eith sat up abruptly and said, "Who do you think that man was? He looked rich."

"I cannot say, I've never seen anyone like any of the people that come in here," I replied weakly.

"Well, for some reason he looked familiar to me... The buttons on his shirt were amber. Did you see them? They sparkled like the morning sun after a stormy night!" she exclaimed, flopping back against the wall with a heavy sigh. "I wish I could have just one tiny piece of amber. It's the most beautiful stone… Is there anything you wish you could have but know you never will, Nika?" Eith looked at me, her big dark blue eyes glimmering with the memories of loss and sadness, her heart clinging to hope and yearning to never have to be alone ever again.

"I wish I could remember what happened after my father sold me, but I may regain those memories. Besides that, the only thing I would do anything to change is to be able to know my mother," I confessed.

Eith's eyes widened and she opened her mouth to say something but at that instant the door behind the counter opened and Malvin emerged with Daon and the man close behind.

"What's this? Being lazy on the job, are we?" he scolded with a wink, hands on hips. "Looks like you two took care of all the hard work for us."

Malvin led the slight-framed man to the front of the shop and shook his jittery hand before the man disappeared. He looked around the shop, void of any customers, and then back to us. "Alright, off you go, just be back before dark."

"We will," Eith beamed, jumping to her feet and yanking me up along with her.

She towed me through the door, down the stairs and the hallway to the back door of the shop. Eith opened a closet I hadn't noticed before that was set into the wall beside the back door and pulled out two long cloaks. She shoved one that was forest green into my hands and clasped one of faded amethyst around her own shoulders. Eith also handed me a circular silver pin the size of my palm with the stamp of a feather pen crossing a small lidded jar.

"What's this?" I asked, giving her a questioning look.

"These bear Malvin's seal, which, by law, prevents all Slavers and Traders from absconding with us when we're away from the shop," she explained, pinning an identical one to the front of her cloak. "The more covert part of Malvin's business is supported by the royal family, so any who cross him also violate their interests."

"I'm sure that makes his job much easier," I guessed, grinning.

"Much easier… Ready?"

I nodded and she unlocked the door with an abundance of clicks and scrapes. She held it open for me to exit first and then shut it behind us, making sure it was pulled securely into its latch.

"There are no keyholes except the first one, how are we supposed to close all the other locks from this side?"

"We don't have to. Daon will come down and make sure the first one is latched in a few minutes. I have a key to get back in and then it's our job to relock all the others when we come back," Eith explained.

She was already bouncing down the alley. I trotted to catch up before she disappeared around the corner, but she stopped and waited where the alley met the street.

"Which way would you like to go? Toward the palace or the wall of the capital?" she asked.

"I saw a bit of the wall when I came to the city, so let's start with the palace," I replied.

"That would be my choice." She snatched my hand and skipped into the street, towing me along behind her into the fray of color.

Eith slowed to a walk after turning onto the street that ran past

Malvin's storefront and we continued side by side. Swept along by a rainbow sea of strangers and eyes wide, I did my best to follow Ned's advice and focus on one incredible thing at a time. Carts of all sizes and shapes passed by on either side of the street; the ones on the right headed toward the center of the city and those on the left moved in the direction of the wall, which was behind us by more blocks than I could even see.

A group of children played a game of skipping stones on one of the doorsteps to the left of the street. A cranky looking little man with wire-rimmed lenses over his eyes yanked the door open and bellowed something at the children in a language I had never heard before.

The children jumped up and scattered into the busy street, dodging between carts. They rushed through the group of people a few feet in front of us, three of them ducking underneath the bellies of two horses drawing a carriage to meet up with the rest of their friends in the alley on the other side of the street.

I gasped as the horses spooked and jittered toward the center of the street, where we were walking. The driver swore and turned them away just in time, then shouted profanity at the children that I also did not understand. The children just started giggling and disappeared into the faint shadows of the alley.

"Don't worry, Nika. All drivers in the city must be approved by the royal family before they start working. There has rarely ever been an accident between a cart driver and pedestrians," Eith said, trying to reassure me with a grin.

"What about those children?" I asked, craning my neck to try and catch a glimpse of them in the alley that we had since passed.

"They are city children. They were born and raised on these streets. They know how to take care of themselves and each other, but they also know how to cause mischief," she shook her head. "Every once in a while, Malvin will have them run errands for him to keep them from vandalizing the shop. Even though they are little ragamuffins, they are the best bet for getting something delivered or retrieved quickly. They know this city as if the streets ran through their veins."

I nodded and then asked, "What were the shop owner and the driver shouting at them?"

"We don't want to know, trust me. Both of them were Muir, from the east, and were speaking Muirsidian," she explained. At my questioning look she continued, "To the east of the Kingdom is the military based Empire of Muirsid. The citizens of Muirsid are oppressed by their government and the land is covered by desolate rock. Most of the lower-middle class people of Muirsid emigrate into the Kingdom or to Linsdiil, the fertile land along the southern border of the Kingdom.

"When my family held East Manor, we saw at least a hundred Muir families migrating through the Eastern Reach and numerous more settling within our Reach each year. There were so many who arrived starving and built themselves up to proud farmers or successful merchants from nothing. It was wonderful and inspiring to see. It gave me strength when I thought all was lost," Eith finished. As we walked, I noticed that she stood a little straighter and held her head a little higher, with the smallest of smiles curving her lips. She looked like the Lady of a Manor.

We continued down the center of the street, gazes fixed on the palace, its domes growing ever closer out of the city with every step. As we came nearer to the palace, the thinner the traffic on the street became. The people and carriages dispersed to different streets before even reaching the wall surrounding the palace grounds.

Eith stopped and turned to me in the center of the nearly deserted road that followed the wall. "There are four entrances to the city and to the palace," she said. "One in honor of each of the four Reaches of the Kingdom. Which Reach did you come from?"

"Northern Reach," I replied.

"Ah, then you would have entered the city by way of the North Gate, since it is much closer to the north than any other entrance to the city. Anyway, there are also four main roads through the city, each one named according to the Gate it is connected to and leads from that Gate directly to the palace. So, luckily, if you get lost it is easy to at least find your way to the nearest main road and then you can just circle the palace until you find your street by following this road," Eith explained the layout of the city and gestured toward the cobbled street in which we were currently standing.

"The people who designed the city must have been very thoughtful," I observed quite lamely, overwhelmed by the wonders of the capital again.

"Well, the first king did employ the most brilliant architects on the Continent, and Jiino as well, to build the city and palace," she agreed.

I was about to ask about Jiino and the first king when the sound of horns rang out from ahead of us.

"Oh, hurry!" Eith exclaimed.

She grabbed my arm and took off at a near sprint toward the commotion and the mob of people crowding the North Palace Gate. Everyone was chattering excitedly as the horns continued to sound. Eith elbowed her way through the crowd, with me in tow, to the open stretch of street. The cobblestones were framed on all sides by city folk and travelers, each face as eager and expectant as the last. Countless necks strained to see above countless heads, attempting to peer through the palace gate.

"Eith, what is going on?" I asked, very confused by the behavior of the surrounding folk.

"This is so exciting! Those horns only sound when the Princes go hunting," she chittered in my ear above the drone of everyone else's muttering.

"Why would they hunt? I doubt they don't have enough food in the palace."

"The only food that is provided in the palace comes from the royal gardens and orchards, as well as the livestock, but the Princes go hunting for their own meat," Eith explained, standing up on her toes.

With a faint whine, the high-arched iron-barred gates slowly glided open and a moment later four mounted guards clattered through the opening, each yelling, "Make way! Make way for the High Princes!" The guards cleared the street as the hunting party exited the courtyard and appeared through the palace gates. The gathered crowd clapped and cheered as the four armored individuals proceeded through the city.

"Each High Prince has his own personal guard handpicked from the ranks. They are the only guards permitted to accompany the Princes absolutely anywhere, and the only ones who participate in hunting," Eith told me, eagerly watching the party inch closer.

The riders sat tall and straight in their saddles. All four wore dark leather bracers and breast plates over light cotton shirts and trousers of browns and greens. The guards' helmets were snug on their heads while the princes carried theirs, eyes trained ahead. The horses' shod hooves clicked on the cobblestone, growing ever louder until I could see the loose, relaxed grip with which the closest guard held his reins. Eith gasped and took a step backward, bumping into me. She looked over her shoulder at me, eyes wide and nervous.

"What is wrong?" I asked, grabbing her elbows to support her shaking body.

"The guard..." she started.

"Which guard?"

"The guard riding next to Prince Kol. There at the front of the procession," she mumbled, pointing to the first of the pairs coming toward us.

"What about him, Eith? Do you know him?" I prodded.

"He... That is Vernier," she choked on the name. "That is my brother."

My mouth fell open and I looked up at the pair riding ever closer. Under the helmet of the Kingdom Guard armor, I could see ebony hair drooping into dark blue eyes. Prince Kol, who rode along the opposite side of the street, cradled what appeared to be a lighter-weight helmet under his left arm. He appeared to be slightly taller than Vernier with dashing features. His hair and eyes were similar in color to those of his personal guard but of a lighter shade.

"What are we going to do? What to do?" Eith muttered incoherently, looking around frantically.

"Wait, what do you mean? You don't want to see your brother?" I asked, spinning her to look at me and holding her tight.

"Yes. No… I don't know what to do. I should have expected him to be here when I heard the horns!" she said, shaking her head. "We should just go back to the shop."

"Eith, why should we?"

"Please, let's just go. Please, Nika!" Her eyes were full of fear and uncertainty.

I couldn't force her to stay, so I led her back the way we came, out and away from the gathered people. I linked my arm through hers and we walked slowly around the palace grounds to the street where Malvin's shop resided. All the way back we walked in silence, and soon her nervous shivers subsided. As we reached the back door of the shop, I turned to Eith to ask for the key but stopped short of asking. Tears were streaming down her cheeks and I could not tell how long she had been crying.

Eith looked up at me, so lost, and asked, "Why am I not strong enough to just speak to him? Or even see him?"

"Oh, Eith," I sighed, pulling her into my arms. She seemed so frail, it was unnerving. "You will speak to him again when the time is right. Of that I have no doubt." We stood in the alley behind Malvin's shop for what seemed like ages. The sun fell below the rooftops in the west, casting us into shadow as crickets began to sing in the waning evening heat.

Pulling away to look into Eith's eyes, I asked, "Shall we go inside now?"

She nodded in response but made no other movements.

"May I have the key so we can?" I reminded her gently.

"Oh, of course!" She reached inside her cloak and pulled out a heavy, slightly rusted iron key. She pressed it into my palm, the handle a metal disc stamped with Malvin's seal. The same one Eith and I wore pinned to our cloaks.

I turned and inserted the key into the lock. It took quite a large amount of wiggling to get it clicked into place, but after only a few minutes of frustration we stood in the back hallway of the shop, as we had earlier that afternoon. Replacing the cloaks and pins where we had found them in the closet earlier, Malvin came tromping down the stairs with Daon not far behind.

"Good evening my lovelies! How went the outing?" he inquired cheerfully.

Eith and I exchanged a look.

"I am going to bed. I'm more tired than I had expected to be," Eith said pitifully. She stepped around us and continued down the hall to her room. "Good night, Malvin, Daon. Sleep well, Nika." She nodded to each of us in turn and disappeared through her door.

"Nika, would you kindly come with me please." Malvin said, his command disguised in the costume of a request. He spun on his heel and stomped up the stairs again.

I looked sideways at Daon but she simply raised her eyebrows. Utterly confused, I followed Malvin's path up the stairs to where he was holding the door to his office open for me. I slipped past his bulk into the too-small room with Daon close behind. Malvin shut the door softly behind us and proceeded around to the opposite side of his desk.

"Please, have a seat, my dear," he gestured toward the finely carved wooden chair across the desk top from him.

I brushed the back of my tunic flat and sat slowly in the chair.

"Now, tell me what happened out there that has left our lovely Eith in such a sorrowful state." Malvin rested his elbows on the desk in front of him, his neck disappearing behind his beard and in between his giant shoulders. If he had not been staring at me so intently, I might have laughed.

"Well..." I hesitated.

"Yes?" he raised and inquiring eyebrow.

"The High Princes were going hunting in the north today, so we went to see them off when the horns sounded. Eith hadn't realized at the time that her brother would be there with Prince Kol," I explained.

"Ah, that makes perfect sense," Malvin sighed, relaxing back in his chair.

"It does?"

"It explains her behavior upon returning tonight. Eith is perfectly sound in mind and body, but the one thing that causes her great distress is the reminder of everything she has lost. Seeing her brother brings those memories to the forefront of her mind, along with everything she longs for," he clarified.

"She also seems to believe that she is not strong enough to face what she has lost," I interjected, "and hates herself for it."

"That is also quite true," he agreed softly, looking at his lap. "This may change some of my plans. I believed Eith had improved since the last chance spotting of her brother."

Malvin murmured something thoughtfully to into his copper-tinged beard, seeming to forget that Daon and I were still in the room.

He took a deep breath and sat up straight in his chair, "Anyway, thank you, Nika, for informing us about this matter. You must be quite tired, so you may retire to your room now, if you would like. As for me, I have some business to attend to, as usual." Malvin stood, smiling broadly, though his eyes were not quite cheery. He waded around the room to the door, where he pulled it open with the most eloquent bow.

I said good night and proceeded down the hall to the stairs and then to my room. There was no noise coming from Eith's room, so I assumed she had fallen asleep. Entering my quarters, I found another fresh apple and part of a loaf of bread resting on the table. I devoured both and flopped onto my small cot, the imminent shadows of sleep approaching quickly.

"Miasma is a last resort. A good idea, but a last resort nonetheless." Restless footsteps paced back and forth on the other side of the door.

"Are you absolutely certain she is necessary, my Lord?"

"Yes! The success of my plan is almost completely contingent on her cooperation, Tenley! Just imagine the power she holds, if only she would accept it! With her under my influence, no one could get in my way. Not even King Lucan and the High Princes!"

There was laughter that sent jolts of fear up my spine and I jerked away from the door as if it had caught fire. I turned and fled down the hall and through the door to the kitchen.

"You were right, Bena! I don't want to believe it, but you're right!" I sobbed, throwing myself into her waiting arms.

7

Business

THE WEATHER BECAME HOTTER and business became busier. Eith and I agreed that we could hear the air outside the shop humming and smell the streets baking. I was completely bewildered by the phenomenon of severe heat, having lived my entire life in the north where the sun was always blocked by trees or hills on a clear day. Eith, on the other hand, moved through her days as if nothing had changed in the last few weeks.

After our outing into the city, Malvin did not let us leave the shop unless he sent us on an errand to retrieve something from one of the other businesses on our street. Every day he said good morning to us then either locked himself in his study, leaving Daon to take care of anything we might need help with, or disappeared into the city with Daon close on his heels. When they went out, they did not return until late in the afternoon, so Eith and I were left to our own devices. Every day I wondered what kind of delicate business Malvin and Daon were attending to that required so much diligent and devoted attention.

This went on for weeks, which turned into a month. In the meantime, we gained another staff member. The poor girl had suffered such a shock by whatever it was that had happened to her that she could not even tell us her name. She was in charge of cleaning the storeroom while we were open and cleaning the front of the shop after hours. I never heard her actually speak, though she did make negative or affirmative sounds and nodded her head yes or no.

It did mean that, because of the new girl's condition, I was moved into Eith's room. Which Malvin and Daon may have discovered was not the best idea since we talked and laughed far too long into the night. In the middle of the second week after our peculiar new addition to the residents of Malvin's shop, there was a soft knock on our door. Eith and I halted our conversation midsentence and simultaneously glanced at the door and then back at each other.

"Come in," Eith called out curiously.

The door opened slowly and Malvin ducked through. Eith and I stood as he came further into the room.

"Malvin, this is a bit of a surprise. Did we wake you?" she asked cautiously.

"No, no, nothing like that, my dears. I have not gone to bed yet," he waved off our concern, taking a seat in the chair against the wall between our cots.

"Is something wrong?" I said. Eith and I sat back down on our cots, her spine just as rigid as mine. Malvin had never come into our rooms before, except for my first morning at the shop, and I could tell the same was true for Eith.

"I just returned from a business meeting at the palace." It was common knowledge that Malvin had business at the palace on a regular basis, but he had never spoken of it before.

"Do we dare ask what that business may have been? Since it apparently has something to do with us," I said cautiously.

"Ah, yes, Nika...always using your head. Something I rather admire about you," Malvin said fondly, giving me a smile. "It is exciting news I believe." He rubbed his hands together nervously and glanced quickly between us.

"Malvin, if it is exciting news, then why are you so worried about it?" Eith asked carefully.

"Eith, you came here when you were fifteen after two years of living with Slavers, and now you are a woman of nineteen. And Nika, I have never in all my years met anyone so mysterious. Unfortunately, neither of you can live the life you were meant to live while you remain here, so these past weeks I have been arranging to transfer your services to the palace."

"Wh-what does that mean? We're leaving?" Eith could barely control the tremor in her voice.

"To put it very bluntly, yes, you are leaving. You have a position as the Princess's personal assistant, and you are expected to begin tomorrow..."

"What about Nika? Will we ever see each other again?" she interrupted.

"...Nika has been accepted as an assistant to the Royal Librarian. She will be going with you to the palace in the morning. That is why the arrangement took so long to be decided. A month ago, it was only Eith who was needed at the palace, but I managed to pull an impressive number of strings so that the two of you would not be separated more than necessary." Malvin finished with an exhalation of breath.

Eith looked at her hands for a moment then said, "But I don't want to leave. I didn't even know the Kingdom had a princess."

"I didn't know either, but that isn't all that surprising," I added, trying to add a little more levity to the conversation.

"The Princess has never left the palace grounds and has been very weak ever since she was born. If you name any known sickness, or unknown for that matter, she has probably had it at one point or another," he informed us.

"How old is she, Malvin?" I asked softly.

"Since you asked, I might as well inform you about the entire royal family. High Prince Kol is the eldest of the four children at twenty-three years; High Prince Ecco is the second child at age twenty; Princess Ranalani is the royal family's treasure who is fifteen, followed by Prince Amr who is just thirteen and a bit of a terror. The High Princes are the sons of the Lucan bloodline who have reached the ruling age, which means they are over eighteen.

"Every king that takes the throne must be a descendant of the first king, who had the surname of Lucan. For simplicity's sake every king's title is King Lucan, but their first names are included when speaking of a specific king."

I stared at Malvin blankly and then glanced at Eith. She looked almost bored. The corners of his mouth quirked up in amusement at my blank look and Malvin continued to explain.

"For example, our current king has always been called King Lucan, correct?"

Eith nodded and I blinked at him.

"All right, his full name is Prentivus Lucan. Those who know him well enough call him King Prentivus but to his subjects he is King Lucan, since the Lucan name holds the real power."

We both nodded and the room fell into silence.

"Are we really leaving tomorrow, Malvin?" I asked quietly.

"I'm afraid you are, my dears," he answered.

"Who will run the shop if both of us are gone?" Eith's wondered.

Malvin laughed at her sincere concern in the question and said, "Well, I suppose Daon and I will have to take care of the storefront for a while, until I find good enough workers again."

After a few minutes of barely any conversation, Malvin took his leave and we snuffed the candles in the room. For a time, the only sounds in the room were the soft rustle of blankets and the faint creak of the shifting boards in the building.

"Nika?"

"What is it Eith?"

"I don't know what to think…"

"Don't think then. We will be fine. We'll still be near each other at least, and that's the important thing. Go to sleep and whatever happens we'll take it on together," I told her bravely.

"You're right of course, as usual." I heard her sigh and roll over on her cot. A few minutes later her soft snoring filled the dark room.

The garden was full of rose bushes in bloom that sprinkled vibrant reds, pinks, and yellows throughout the tall straight trees. The dark wood contrasted with the brightness of the flowers while the glittering glass walls and ceiling blocked the cold wind that whistled outside. The heat of the sun was still fresh from the day before inside the glass enclosure.

The polite and playful aromas of the roses and the spicy tang of the needles on the trees tickled my nose as I waded through the abundant emerald ferns that filled in the gaps between the trees. The fronds slipped across the slightly coarse satin of my royal blue skirt like caressing fingers as I strolled toward the tiny sparkling pond hidden from sight by the lavish foliage.

I trailed my hand softly across the open rose buds as I walked, the calloused skin of my fingers jealous of the velvet petals. Perhaps I could pick some of them for a bouquet. Bena told me she loved roses of any kind, but rarely got the chance to enjoy them.

"There you are, my joy!" his voice echoed through the courtyard, causing me to squeal and spin in a panicked circle until strong hands tenderly gripped my shoulders.

"I've told you not to do that!" I sucked in a large breath as the tension melted from my limbs, leaving them loose and tingling. Heat flared in my cheeks as his laugh rang in my ears, his eyes flashing yellow.

"It's not funny. Stop it," I said, wriggling out of his grasp. I folded my arms across my stomach as I resumed my walk.

"Relax, my dear. It's just a little bit of fun," he replied. "You know I just like to play with you."

I gave him the courtesy of a sideways glare as he followed me. "Yes, I do know that, but the point you seem to ignore is that even though some things are fun for you, they may not be fun for others. Besides, it gives me this creepy feeling all up my spine and I don't like it."

"Very well, I will rein in my impulses," he sighed.

"Thank you." I dropped my arms and tilted my chin toward the tops of the trees. Between the branches I could see fragments of dark, angry clouds on the other side of the glass. There would be a storm that night. I could feel it in my bones.

He and I strolled in silence for a few minutes as I resumed my appreciation of the courtyard that was all my own. I thought reverently, I never would have hoped for anything like this. From dirty rags to satin and warm wool dresses…

"Nika, what are you thinking about?"

"Hm? Oh, nothing really," I replied.

"I know you were thinking about something. I could see it in your eyes. Don't lie to me." There was an irritated rumble in his throat that laced his words with a warning. Prickles danced up my back and into the base of my skull. He calmly looped my right hand through his bent arm, but I could feel the tension coursing through his muscles.

"I…was just thinking how I've miraculously gone from a miner's daughter living in a filthy, run down village to this," I said, waving my free arm in a gesture meant to encompass the entire Manor.

"Ah, is that so?" His body relaxed and he returned to his usual, gentlemanly self.

"I said it was nothing important," I muttered to the ground.

He brought our slow walk to a halt and took my hands in both of his. "My dear, every thought and truth that each person brings to light is more important than the stars in the sky. Do not doubt the power of thoughts or that, despite being a destitute miner's daughter, you are radiant in any guise."

I stared at him blankly for a moment, then said slowly, "You amaze me, my Lord. I believe you are not all that you seem."

"That, Miss Fobess, would be a very astute observation." Once more he looped my hand through his elbow, and we resumed walking. "I just hope you do not despise what I wholly am."

His words were so soft and careful that I had no response. Instead, a particularly full rose blossom caught my attention and I quickened our pace toward it. The rose bush had more tendrils than the rest of the bushes and overflowed into the path. I stepped around many of the unruly branches to cradle the bloom in my cupped hands.

"Isn't this beautiful? Wouldn't Bena love it?"

"I'm sure she would. Just be careful of those thorns. It looks as though the gardener hasn't finished his job here and this bush seems much spinier than the others," he warned.

I glanced at the branches of the bush and noticed the thorns that were unusually large for most roses. They were half as long as my little finger.

"I'm always careful," I said jovially, giving him a light smile over my shoulder. I plucked the bloom from its stem and turned slowly, avoiding the long green branches as best I could. Seemingly clear, I exclaimed, "See, no trouble," and took a step forward.

The skirt of my dress stopped me mid step, pulling me off balance. The thorny branches low to the ground snagged the hem of my skirt and my momentum forward shifted sideways. The world tipped and just before I hit the ground, the tiny spears tore through the fabric around my waist. Lord Rafas reached for me as though in slow motion, and then the hard-packed dirt slammed into me.

A hundred knife points gouged the skin from my right hip and along my back to the base of my neck. A scream of pain tore from my throat, followed by another and another as my spine turned to liquid fire. The bones in my shoulders crunched into a new shape that ripped through my slashed skin. From the tops of my feet to the base of my ears, it felt like miniscule razor blades pushed their way out of my bones and through muscle and skin, one right on top of another.

Through the haze of red I heard people shouting and running. They sounded like they were far away, but all that mattered was the pounding in my head and the raging pulse of my blood.

8
Change

SOMEONE WAS KNOCKING very loudly on the door.

"Rise and shine my lovelies!" Malvin called through the wood. "We have an appointment for an hour past daybreak, and we really shouldn't be late."

Eith groaned from the other side of the room. She rolled over and looked at me as we heard Malvin stomp back up the stairs.

"In other words, get your lovely rears in action," she grumbled.

I stifled a burst of laughter and ended up gagging on it. Eith grinned, her eyes cloudy with sleep.

We pulled our tunics on over our linen shifts and crunched on our usual breakfast of an apple and bread. With one hand on the door knob, Eith turned and cast a lingering gaze around the room. The middles of the tightly made cots curved inward just barely and the lightly scuffed planks of the floor made the room look well-used and cared for.

"It will be strange sleeping somewhere else again. Just like I thought when I first came here," she said softly. "It's interesting how life changes things. You and I are proof of that." She smiled at me briefly and then opened the door.

Daon stood in the hallway, holding the faded amethyst and forest green cloaks that Eith and I had worn before. She handed us the cloaks, her expression unreadable.

"I will tell Tuscal you are ready. Today you do not need his marks to go out into the city since he will be with you," she said simply. We watched her climb the stairs and turn down the hall to Malvin's office.

"Do you know why she always calls him Tuscal?" I asked Eith.

"I believe it is just her way."

I made a neutral sound in acknowledgement as Daon came back down the stairs, preceded by Malvin. He wore a cloak similar to ours that was a rich wine red in color and appeared to be made of velvet. Thin copper rope framed its edges and ran in loops and swirls around the column of four silver buttons that clasped the cloak around Malvin's broad chest.

"My, don't you look official," Eith teased, placing a fist on her hip.

"I try to look professional when I need to," he said sheepishly, a blush barely hidden beneath his beard. "Are we ready, girls?" He straightened his clothing, recovering from the unexpected complement.

"I think we're ready," I answered, glancing at Eith.

"As ready as we'll ever be, I guess," she added with a nervous smile.

"In that case, shall we?" Malvin gestured with a shallow bow toward the multi-lock back door that Daon had managed to open without Eith or myself noticing. "Daon will close the door behind us and open the shop for me while I'm out."

I followed Eith down the hall and through the door into the waxing morning light. The air had a strong aroma of oranges and the various other citrus that were grown on the Capital Lands outside the city wall. Once outside, we waited a moment for Malvin to give Daon some instructions and close the door behind us.

When Malvin was ready, we took the same path Eith and I had taken toward the palace weeks before. The street that led to the East Palace Gate was just as busy, despite the early hour of the morning. We dodged carriages and carts as well as early bird shoppers and city children causing havoc in the streets.

At the iron-barred gate, Malvin simply said, "Wait here," and went to speak to one of the guards. There was a pair on either side of the gate, watching the length of street before them as far as they could see.

The details on the guards' armor were exquisite. Their breastplates bore the symbol of the Kingdom, like the image above the main gate of the capital. A brilliant golden sun rested in the middle of their chests, surrounded by intricate vines that wound their way across the shoulder guards and down the armored plates on the thighs of each guard. The armor was made of flawless iron and shone silver, except for the sun on the guards' chests which looked as though each one could radiate gilded sunlight.

The guard Malvin was speaking to shouted over his shoulder and a moment later the gate swung open. Malvin motioned for us to follow and we hurried after him. The gate was closed with resounding clang immediately after we passed through.

Eith and I stopped in our tracks. We were surrounded by a wide circular courtyard lined with exotic trees and ferns of varying shades of green. The stones under our feet were placed so close together that the ground seemed as though it was solid rock. Directly across the courtyard were gigantic wooden double doors with crystal windows set in their center. The wood was pale as white sand and looked sturdy as stone. The edges of the windows were framed by the same vines as those on the Main Gate and at the doors' apex was the sun of the Kingdom.

Above the doors, rose the palace itself. Wherever there weren't sparkling windows, was pale wood under sky-colored paint and the occasional stone column in the corners. Its domed crystal roofs made it look like something of myth or out of a fantastic fairytale.

"Come along then!" Malvin called to us from the far side of the courtyard, standing before the beautiful double doors. The doors dwarfed the giant man almost comically.

We shuffled across the stones to where he waited. What I had neglected to notice previously were the two guards stationed in front of the doors. As we approached, they grasped the large cast iron ring that served as the handle to one of the doors and heaved. Together they slowly managed to pull the door open, scraping it across the ground. Upon entering, the door was gradually shoved closed behind us.

"We are expected in the throne room, and it would be best if you two stayed close," Malvin said seriously to our bewildered faces. "It is in the center of the palace and I would hate for either of you to get lost along the way."

He started off down the corridor and we did our best to keep up with his long strides. Each corridor was equally as impressive as the last and the ceilings were even higher than the tops of the doors by which we had entered the palace. Everywhere I looked there was something remarkable.

We followed the corridor that ran along an outside wall of the palace, which was almost entirely windows along one side. When we turned onto an inner corridor that led to the center of the palace the walls were pale wood from floor to ceiling. The ceilings of the halls were also wood, but some had intricate paintings of nature or abstract scenes spanning their surfaces and even spilling down the walls to join the elegant weavings that lined the corridors.

All the important doors in the palace appeared to be identical. The doors to the throne room looked the same as the doors to the East Courtyard and I would soon find out that the doors to the four different Wings of the palace were also of the same design. Unlike the doors in the courtyard, though, the doors to the throne room were open and the fine film of dust on the floor near their base indicated that they had not been closed for a long time.

If the expansive throne room ceiling was any example, then the domes of the palace were not half-spheres but made out of rounded squares or rectangles fit together. My gaze lowered to where the walls met the glass ceiling and my mouth hung open at the intricate and detailed ivy that ringed the room. Whoever had painted those leaves and vines had been so skilled that the plants seemed to be living. Tiny white and silver jasmine flowers dotted the vines, showing their faces like bright stars among the rich green ivy.

Weavings of scenes even more impressive than those in the corridors lined the walls of the throne room. An entire oak tree sprouted from the center of the room, cracking a few of the stones that created the floor of the palace. The branches reached up to the glistening roof and the base of the tree was partly hollowed out into the shape of a rough chair. The edge of a huge map of the Continent and Jiino could just barely be seen around the trunk of the tree.

"Malvin, my good man, lovely to see you again so soon!" a voice boomed through the air.

I jumped, bumping into Eith and she nervously linked her arm with mine.

"Ah, Prentivus, there you are! Making an entrance, as usual, I see," Malvin replied.

He grinned and crossed the space to embrace the man who had appeared from behind the tree. We scurried along behind him at a respectable and safe distance. After a few words of greeting were exchanged, Malvin turned to us.

"These are the magnificent young ladies you have managed to steal off of me, my friend, Eith Liffei and Nika Fobess." He gestured to Eith and I in turn and we each made a slight bow. "This is his majesty, King Prentivus Lucan."

I did my best to keep my eyes from popping out of my head and clasped my hands together to keep them from shaking. We were in the presence of the King. There was a faint energy that seemed to radiate off his skin and there was a twist in my gut that told me he was more than simply what meets the eye. He was not a young man and, if I looked closely, I could see arthritis starting to take a toll on his strong hands. His back wasn't as straight as it once had been, and his light-colored hair had faded to creamy silver. I was interested to see that King Prentivus wore no crown.

"Malvin, you scoundrel. You failed to mention how absolutely lovely they are," the King scolded playfully, stepping forward and bringing first my hand and then Eith's to his lips in respectful greeting.

Both of our jaws dropped to the floor. His eyes were a slate gray that appeared to shimmer and glisten, making something twinge in the back of my mind.

"Come into my more private reception area," he extended his arm toward the map and we hesitantly followed his instructions.

On the back side of the magnificent tree was another rough, seat-shaped carving, hollowed out of the tree's giant trunk. The map was framed on either side by a curved staircase that led up to the mysterious second story of the palace.

"Now," King Prentivus said as he took his place on the throne at the back of the tree, "did I hear Malvin say one of you was a Liffei?"

Eith stared at him, frozen by shock. I glanced her way and nudged her with my foot.

"I-I am Eith Liffei, your majesty," she managed quietly with a shaky curtsy.

"No need to be nervous, Miss Liffei. I believe there is someone currently living under my roof that would be delighted to know that you are here. In fact, I even authorized a six week leave from the guard so that he could search the whole of the Eastern Reach and half of the Northern Reach, all the way to the Moving Mountains," he said nonchalantly, although I could see the spark in his eyes. "Your father's death was upsetting, and the abduction tragic. Especially for Vernier..." His majesty let that settle, obviously knowing more than he was saying.

"Anyway, on a different note, first things first, which is business," the king exclaimed, rising from his seat and striding across the space to where a long, broad table covered in papers rested against the wall. "Malvin, these are the transfer papers. You need to sign the bottom next to where I have already signed." Prentivus handed Malvin a pamphlet and he began to shuffle through it as the king opened a case of quills and unstopped the crystal ink bottle that rested elegantly on a corner of the table.

"Miss Liffei, you may be interested to know that this transaction would not be taking place if Sars Rafas were actually contacting us or even answering our queries. The yearly trainees of each of the Manors were due weeks ago but we haven't heard anything from the Eastern or Northern Reaches. The Southern and Western Reaches both sent us stable hands, which we need very much," he informed Eith, making conversation as Malvin scratched his name on the pertinent pages. The king got a thoughtful, distant look on his face and added half to himself, "I get the feeling that I will regret giving two Reaches to Lord Rafas, even if the arrangement is temporary."

Each time I heard the name Rafas my heart and stomach wrenched painfully. The thought shot through my mind, *That man is a monster*, though I didn't exactly know why. Malicious golden eyes flashed across my vision and I stifled a gasp, the memory of slashing claws rushing to the front of my mind. My back began to tingle and burn, my panic causing my body to react to the memories. I took a deep breath and looked up into Eith's worried, steady gaze. I managed a small smile that seemed to assuage her concern for the moment. Luckily neither King Prentivus nor Malvin seemed to have noticed my brief episode.

"Would you care to inspect my signatures, Prentivus?" Malvin asked. He turned his back on the table where he had been writing and offered the pamphlet to the king.

"I don't believe it is necessary, my friend," the king answered with a smile. "Thank you so much for everything." Prentivus took the papers and set them back on the table, clasping Malvin's arm in fondness and friendship. "You may be on your way if you wish."

"Very well, I wish I could stay much, much longer, but I have more business to take care of back at the shop," Malvin said regretfully. He turned to us. "My dears, I plan on seeing you within the next couple weeks and I do hope both of you find what it is you are searching or yearning for, either here or elsewhere." He pulled us both into the epitome of a bear hug, bowed to the king and was on his way with a proud but sad expression.

"Shall we introduce you to your new positions, ladies?" King Prentivus asked, walking past us toward the doors. It wasn't much of a question, but niceties are better than none. We crossed the huge room, the tree dominating the space behind us, and exited into another hallway.

Following close on the king's heels, he led us down the corridor and stopped outside grand double doors at the intersection of two outer corridors where windows lined the walls. The guards on either side of the doors bowed and then one of them heaved a door open. He quickly stepped through and spoke to someone on the other side briefly. When he returned to his post, he bowed again and gestured for us to enter.

The king swept through the door while Eith and I gave each other a look and then followed. The room on the other side was so beautiful I didn't know whether to weep or giggle, so I simply stared. The floors were identical to those in the rest of the palace but only half of the room had wooden walls. The room itself was circular and the far side was entirely glass, including the ceiling. Through the windows we could see row upon row of exotic, wild gardens.

"My darling, how are you feeling today?" the king said enthusiastically.

He was standing over a girl younger than me and most certainly smaller in stature. She sat in a wooden rocking chair laden with fluffy blankets. Her skin was unusually pale, but not sickly, and wisps of light sandy hair framed her face. She noticed our hesitation and motioned for us to come closer.

"I am fine today, Father. I'm simply resting. Who have you brought me?" she answered the king.

As we approached, I noticed her eyes were bright green and unsettlingly similar to mine, though at a second glance I saw the ring of brown around her pupils.

"These are our newest residents, Eith and Nika. Eith is your new attendant," he told her. "Girls," he said, addressing us, "this is my daughter, Princess Ranalani."

We bowed and the princess inclined her head to us.

"Sire?" a voice called from the doorway. A thin, grizzled man with glasses and a sheaf of papers stood just inside the threshold. I recognized him as the man with amber buttons who Malvin had met with in the shop. I nudged Eith and she nodded.

"I must be off, but I trust you can have someone show Nika to the library, my dear," the king said to his daughter.

"Of course, Father."

The king kissed her forehead then hurried out of the room.

"Will you kindly help me up? They always pile the furniture so high with pillows and blankets that I just sink into them and get stuck. It's not like I'll shatter if I sit on wood, you know." Princess Ranalani raised her arms, wanting us to take her hands. Eith and I smiled, pulling her out of the chair. She was surprisingly tall for how little she seemed while seated.

A faint, pulsing energy tickled against my palm when I took her hand. It was the same kind of energy that I had felt around the king, but hers was hidden in her bones rather than emitted into the air. I didn't understand how I knew it was in her bones, but I just did. My mountain of questions was getting higher with every person I met in the capital, and I needed answers.

"Now that my attendant is here, I can go outside. It takes two to carry the umbrella." She crossed the room and opened a wardrobe next to the gracefully carved four-poster bed. The princess pulled out a folded umbrella that had two handles peeking out from under the thick dark fabric. She untied the string that held it closed and yanked the handles in opposite directions. The contraption popped open and, like everything else in the palace, it was huge. It was nearly the size of the bed, which could have held three people shoulder to shoulder.

"Um, your highness, may I ask you something?" Eith asked politely.

"Of course, and please call me Rani. There are two things I despise. The first is formality and the second is obnoxious noises," the princess replied.

"Why do you need such a large, heavy umbrella?"

"That has a simple answer: I am allergic to sunlight. If I go outside in the sun it makes me sick," she answered simply. "Are you going to help me with this thing?"

Eith rushed over and helped her lift the umbrella over their heads. Elation plain on the princess's face, she led Eith toward the doors and I assumed I was expected to follow them. The guards did not bow as we exited.

Ranalani said with a grin, "All of the guards know not to bow to me. It drives Father crazy."

The princess talked incessantly as we walked down the hall.

"I would like to introduce you to my brothers, but two of them are currently away from the palace on business for my father and Amr is no fun when he's interrupted from fawning over the horses."

She made intricate gestures with her free hand as she spoke, as though her arm and fingers were tracing an image just as clearly as the words that rolled off her tongue.

"For now, I suppose I should send Nika to the library. Be a good girl and do as Father asks and all that." She sighed and called one of the guards to show me the way to the library. "We shall all see each other soon."

With a radiant smile, she turned on her heel and continued to march along the corridor. Eith glanced quickly back at me with a bemused look in her eyes as I watched them go. I stood stock still, reminiscing about how I had imagined a princess would be slightly different.

"To the library then?" the guard at my elbow asked. He was probably a few years older than Eith.

I nodded and he led the way.

The library also had double doors, but they were about half the size of the others. The rich chestnut wood was etched with beautiful roses and foreign runes. The guard opened the door for me and politely said farewell to return to his post.

As I entered, the first thing that caught my eye was the lighting in the library. The crystal ceiling was tinted the tiniest bit darker than the other windows I had seen, probably to protect the contents of the library from sun damage. There were flickering metal lanterns dangling from hooks fixed to the shelves, the light of one lantern beginning where the light of the previous one ended. The center of the room was filled with tables covered in manuscripts and writing utensils. Around the edges were innumerable head-high bookcases that were dwarfed by the shelves that lined the walls from floor to ceiling. On each wall was a sliding ladder fixed to the top of the shelving.

At that moment one of the ladders glided around the edge of the room and came to a stop abruptly on my right. I jumped to the side a step and craned my neck to see the top of it.

"Hello, can I help you with something?" a voice drifted down from near the rafters, where a woman was facing me, walking down the rungs of the ladder. She seemed to be floating in the air. "Well? Don't just stand there and gawk."

I realized my mouth was rudely hanging open and I snapped it shut. This woman looked nearly identical to Daon, though her face wasn't as severe.

When she reached the ground and was standing in front of me, I managed, "I'm, uh, supposed to be the new library assistant."

"Wonderful, you're just in time! We got in a new collection of old volumes that need to be organized by subject and alphabetized," she exclaimed, clapping her hands together. "I've been slaving away on them since yesterday, but first let's get you settled in a bit."

She strode straight back into the depths of the library, weaving through the free-standing bookshelves. My mind whirling, I scurried after her.

She led the way through a small door into what appeared to be an alcove of the library. The door was nestled in a pale wooden wall that looked to have been built more recently than the rest of the library. The wall and the door were covered in shelves full of books, just like the rest of the room.

The room on the other side of the door was tiny compared to the library but was still twice as large as my room at Malvin's. It was furnished like a bedroom but had two of everything placed at comfortable intervals. The living space closest to the door had a collection of personal items among the generic furniture. Unlike the rest of the palace, aside from the throne room, the walls were solid gray stone.

"The bed towards the back is yours. My previous assistant got married six months ago, so she has a new home now. Although she has come to visit now and then," the woman said kindly. "Oh, how rude of me, my name is Wynna." She extended her hand in formal greeting.

"I am Nika," I said, clasping her hand.

"Well, I look forward to working with you, Nika. Take a look at your new living quarters and when you're ready come find me in the library. I'll probably be up a ladder," she grinned, winked, and then disappeared through the door.

I went to the back of the room and sat on the bed, which was much more comfortable than I was used to. The feather mattress was raised off of the floor on a polished wood frame. A bedside table sat next to it with a small, latched door on the front and a glass lamp resting on its smooth top. In the very back corner was a large wardrobe. It was the only one in the room and it was much too large for only one person. At the end of each bed there was a thick, wooden chest with an iron lock holding the lid firmly closed.

I unclasped my forest green cloak and laid it on the bed. Exiting the library living quarters, I went to find the Royal Librarian. She was dangling off the side of the ladder where I had first seen her with an ancient-looking book in one hand and a stack of them balanced on the other. I guessed she was placing some of the new arrivals.

"Wynna, just how long have you been the Royal Librarian?" I called up to her.

"Hm? Oh, about twenty years I suppose, give or take a few," she said idly, glancing down at me over her shoulder as she easily slid a thick volume into place.

I watched as she continued up the ladder without using her hands, placing books in their rightful places along the way. By the time she reached the rim of the crystal ceiling she had placed the final book from her stack. A few moments later she stood in front of me grinning.

"It would probably be more accurate to give a few years though. Shall I show you around our wonderful library?"

I followed as she went to the center of the giant room and turned her back on the doors. I stood at her elbow and followed her gaze to a balcony that I was surprised I hadn't noticed before.

"The king can look over the whole library from there. When he needs information on a specific subject, he hollers for me to find it and bring it up to him," she said.

"What is on the second floor of the palace?" I asked.

"Well, the throne room and the library are the only two-story rooms in the palace, but the second-floor wraps around those two areas. The southern end is home to the king's quarters and the eastern side is where all of the royal offices are located. Also, oddly enough, the western side houses the guest and laundry rooms."

"Laundry rooms?" I said, incredulously.

"I suppose the king likes to be near his laundry, or there was just nowhere else to put it after filling up the first floor," Wynna shrugged.

She walked to the back of the room again, this time on the opposite side from the living space. The wall was covered in books, just like the rest of the library, but Wynna stepped forward pulled back the corner of a massive weaving that only looked like shelves full of books.

"That is amazing," I said absently, still staring, and completely dumbfounded.

"I know. This is my favorite part of the library. Come on, I can't hold this up forever," she beckoned, grasping the hanging over one shoulder. I hurried past her and she let the weaving drop, plunging us into total darkness.

"Wynna?" I said, confused as I heard her scratching around for something in the dark.

"One moment… aha!"

The plain brown backside of the wall hanging was suddenly illuminated by a lantern in Wynna's hand. She circled the room, lighting the lanterns lining the walls. I traced her steps slowly, marveling at how many of the volumes on the shelves were even still intact. Some were severely water damaged while others looked like wild animals had attempted to eat them.

"This is what we like to call the Archive," Wynna said. She stood in the center of the triangular room and held the lantern above her head. "Every book in the Kingdom that holds particularly unusual information or value is stored here, and our primary purpose is to protect it at all costs."

"If they are so valuable, why not have guards posted on the library?"

"Guards have a rather unfortunate habit of drawing attention to themselves and those near them," she sighed. "Plus, if we make people believe these don't even exist," she raised her free hand, gesturing to the shelves, "then we won't have to guard it too closely, if at all."

"We're still in the library, but why is the ceiling here and in the bedroom lower and made of stone?" I wondered.

"Technically we're underneath the stairs that lead to the upper level. That would be the simple, short answer without going into the history of the palace. That, my friend, is for another time." She carefully went to each lantern and snuffed the flames, saving the one in her hand for last. After she lifted the hanging again, light from outside drifting in through the gap, Wynna doused the final lantern and rehung it on the wall inside the Archive. I ducked through and she let the weaving fall into place behind her.

"Now," she said, rubbing her palms on the front of her dress, "let's get started on those new books. Lead the way back to the tables, please." She gave me an encouraging smile. I turned toward the center of the room and the soles of my sandals tapped on the stone floor.

Wynna pointed me toward the tables occupying the west side of the room, which were completely covered in volumes from the size of my palm to as large as my chest.

"How many are there?" I asked in amazement.

"Once they're all sorted and placed, we'll have a number. At the beginning of each year I have to check the inventory of the library, which means counting all the books and making sure they are the same as what is logged," she said. "Every once in a while, I'll find a few that I have never seen before, at which point it gets interesting."

All of the books had already been sorted by subject, so all that was left was alphabetizing. When noon came around, we took a break and ate the delicious food one of the kitchen aids brought us. Wynna made sure a table was emptied and the food was nowhere near any of the books or manuscripts.

For the rest of the day, we organized enough volumes to clear off a couple tables and parts of others. We knew it was dusk when the only light in the library came from the numerous lanterns.

"I think that's enough for today. Would you carefully douse the lanterns on the lower shelves while I take care of the ones up high?" Wynna asked, slouching in her chair.

"Of course," I said.

"Take them down and hold them away from the books before you blow them out, please," she sighed, slowly getting up and going to the nearest ladder.

I did as she asked and when only one lantern was left alight, Wynna drew a large iron key from her skirt pocket. She went to the double doors and there was an audible clack as the lock slid heavily into place. Then she turned and led me through the shelves once again to the bedroom.

We both fell onto our individual beds. My mind was whirling so terribly that I barely had time to get underneath the covers and mutter, "I should warn you that I have bad dreams," before the velvety darkness of sleep took over.

I sat at a long, narrow table. At least twenty people could have eaten there at the same time, but only four places were set, which had been the case every night for the past seven months. Tenley sat as far away from me as possible, his usual arrogant expression frozen in place.

Bena entered through a side door, hefting a large covered tray in both hands. It smelled wonderful. Lord Rafas had gone hunting that morning and brought back at least twenty fat quail, more than enough for our small household to enjoy for a few nights.

She plopped the tray on the table and uncovered its contents. Inside were four of the surprisingly large birds surrounded by steamed carrots, beets, and sliced squash. Bena took her seat on my right, across from Tenley, and a few moments later the missing member of our group entered.

"Good evening, I haven't missed too much I hope," Lord Rafas greeted us cheerfully.

"Bena just revealed the dinner, sir," Tenley replied haughtily.

"Wonderful! It certainly looks magnificent, as always, Bena," he exclaimed, gently touching his lips to the top of my head before taking his seat across from me.

I carefully masked a disgusted shiver and shoved the thought of our earlier argument aside. The bruise on my face throbbed and my fingers itched to hide it even though it no longer showed.

"Thank you, my Lord," Bena replied quietly.

"Shall we begin? Does everyone have their glasses?" Lord Rafas asked, picking up a bottle of wine. He poured himself, Tenley, and Bena some wine and then opened a bottle of apple cider for me, as was the normal routine. "Tenley, would you mind doing the honors?"

Tenley made an unhappy but affirmative noise and began to serve our meal. Everyone took a turn or two during the week.

I inelegantly took a gulp of my cider, hoping it would calm my agitated stomach. Lord Rafas's close proximity made my insides roll.

Avoiding his gaze like the plague, I managed to get through almost half of my dinner before something changed. All evening I had been fixated on avoiding him, but I wasn't sure why any more. What was the reason that

I had so disliked even the thought of him?

My hard thinking must have shown on my face because Lord Rafas asked, "Are you feeling alright, my joy?"

"Oh yes, I'm perfectly fine," I answered, slightly startled.

"Good, would you like something more to drink?" He poured me another glass of cider, which I took and gulped half of it.

Why was my throat so dry all of a sudden? I downed the rest in one swallow. My skin was burning under his gaze, forcing me to look up into his face. I stared at his handsome features and shocking eyes.

Why would I ever defy him?

9
Questions

"WYNNA!" a voice broke through the edges of sleep...

"Wynna!!" It became much louder, like the blast of a horn. My eyes snapped open, heart racing. I thought I recognized it as the voice of the king but could not be sure through the stone walls.

Across the room, Wynna groaned and swung out of bed. Pulling a faded blue tunic over her night clothes, she stumbled out into the library. I sat up and could hear muffled conversation on the other side of the door.

Moments later Wynna reentered our quarters with a sigh and said, "The king is requesting very specific reading material, which I must retrieve for him from the shelves. I tend to stay with the king to aid him in finding the pertinent information, so if you could continue alphabetizing the remaining books that would be very helpful."

"Of course," I replied with a yawn.

"Apparently King Prentivus is up to an early start this morning... Anyway, just make sure the subject material doesn't get mixed up," she advised, half out the door with a curious look on her face.

I slid out of bed and noticed two unfamiliar tunics that lay folded neatly on the chest at the end of the bed. Both were ankle-length and sleeveless. One was a light green while the other was an intriguing burgundy color. I took a glance at my worn, no longer cream-colored tunic that sat beside them on the top of the chest. Without a second thought, I pulled the pale green one over my head. I brushed my hands over the front of it, enjoying its crisp, clean scent and smooth texture.

For hours I sifted through piles of leather-bound parchment containing more information than I could possibly imagine. At least half of the volumes were written in other languages, containing rows of mysterious symbols that nearly made me go cross eyed.

I continued to use the method that Wynna had explained to me the day before. I went from one table to the next, organizing the titles that started with the same letter, then when someone else took over they could simply be told what letter to start with. Also, if Wynna were moving the sorted books to the shelves, then she could take the ones of all the same alphabetical persuasion and we wouldn't have to go back to letters that had already been dealt with.

Just before the sun reached its zenith overhead, I was half way through the M's at the table of particularly rare and mythical subjects. For some reason all of the books I needed were at the bottom of the heap.

There was one simple, water-worn volume just slightly larger than my hand that seemed out of place. I reached for it but when my fingers came within a few inches of its cover, it was as though the book emitted an electrical field. My hand and forearm were riddled with audible and tangible silver sparks. I squealed in surprise, yanking my hand away from the book and taking a few hasty steps backward.

I cradled my arm against my chest, warily regarding the plain little book from a safe distance. I watched as the silver sparks retreated back under its cover. One of the long, thin wooden tools that were used to turn the pages of tomes that were too fragile to touch caught my eye. Grabbing it off of the nearby table, I slowly moved closer to the book, brandishing the tool in front of me like a weapon. I carefully wiggled the tip of the tool underneath the cover and slowly pried the book open. The writing on the first page was made up of letters that I knew from my own language, but I could not understand the words they spelled out.

MAWYL: TAH SISAND TAHN AF TAH LYUKIAN RESIZ

The doors of the library opened and closed with a click and a bang. I jumped, dropping the tool and spinning around quickly. I breathed a sigh of relief when I saw it was only Wynna and attempted to calm my racing heartbeat.

"How goes the alphabetizing, Nika?" she asked wearily, plopping down in a nearby chair.

"A book attacked me, but I'm half finished with M," I informed her.

"Wh-what?!" she sputtered, her eyes going wide. "A *book* attacked you?"

"It sent shocks into my hand and up my arm when I touched it."

She stared at me blankly for a minute. "Where is it?"

I pointed to where the book still lay with its front cover open. After a moment Wynna stood and went to the table, bending this way and that to examine the appearance of the book and then she squinted at the words on the first page.

"Do you know what it means?" I asked eagerly, moving to her side.

"I have seen language like this before..." she replied. "There are two books identical to this one in the Archives, but the titles are different. I never gave them much thought." She reached out both hands and scooped the little book off of the table. There was no reaction whatsoever.

"Why did it shock me and not you?"

"I could not say. None of the others ever reacted to me either," she answered, her thoughts far away. "Come with me." Wynna took off at a brisk walk toward the Archives and I did my best to keep up.

Once we were inside and all the lanterns had been lit, she gingerly placed the book on one of the two large tables in the center of the room. She went to the farthest corner of the room, where two of the walls came together at a sharp angle, intently searching the shelves. I stood aimlessly by the table, a safe distance from the book whose cover I was afraid would begin crackling at any moment.

"Aha!" Wynna exclaimed, brandishing two very similar books above her head as she came back to the table. She laid the new tomes alongside the other. They were identical, except for the letters inscribed on their spines.

"Do you think these will shock me too?" I asked warily.

"Maybe, but I don't know," Wynna shrugged. "There's one way to find out."

"Oh no. No, no. I'm not touching any of them." I waved my hands back and forth.

"I won't make you touch them, don't worry," Wynna chuckled.

I gave a sigh of relief and stepped closer to the table, reading the titles of the other books.

KYLTH: TAH FERST TAHM AF TAH LYUKIAN RESIZ

LYKKE: TAH THIRD TAHM AF TAH LYUKIAN RESIZ

"What language is that?" I asked. "Can you understand what it says?" I turned to Wynna expectantly. She was the Royal Librarian after all.

"I'm afraid I do not know," she replied.

My shoulders slumped as I looked down at the mysterious little books.

"I do know where we can find out though," Wynna added with a wise smile.

She placed the books together on the shelf in the corner. I helped her douse the lights then followed her through the wall hanging and across the library to the shelves that surrounded the door to our quarters.

"Every language that has ever been spoken within the borders of the Continent and Jiino lie in the pages of these books," Wynna said. "It might take a while to find exactly what we're looking for though, since we don't know what it's called."

"I had no idea there were so many languages," I said softly, gawking at the shelves of books.

"Well, they aren't all completely different languages. Many are very ancient variations of languages we know today," she explained. "A few of them have multiple volumes, and each language is described in exquisite detail. Some are even simply the history and evolution of a language."

"These are beautiful..." I trailed my fingers across the spines of the books closest to me. They were bound in richly colored and textured fabrics. The titles pressed into the spines had been accentuated by gold or silver ink, though many of the words and symbols were faded and crumbling off of the surfaces of the volumes. When I carefully slid one of them halfway off of the shelf, I discovered delicate filigree designs that swirled across the cover.

"Many of the most stunning books I have ever seen are on these particular shelves. I'm glad I'm not the only one of that opinion."

I glanced over at Wynna. She was smiling fondly at the neat rows in front of her. The adoration for her work glimmered in her eyes. After a moment she took a sharp breath and turned to me.

"We should finish sorting those other books before we get too sidetracked."

"What about that language? Shouldn't we find out what it is?"

"Yes, we should," she said, nodding slowly, "that is part of a librarian's job, but we will have plenty of time for that after the more pressing work is done. Now, let's finish placing the rest of the new arrivals. I don't believe there are too many left to put away."

Wynna turned on her heel and clipped back to the center of the library. I followed close behind her and carried out her instructions for the rest of the day, but my mind was constantly drawn back to the mysterious little volumes that apparently had a dislike for me. Whenever I thought of them a tingling would start in my fingers and stealthily creep its way up my arms into the back of my neck. I would shiver and shake it off, forcing myself to focus on the instructions that Wynna was chattering in my ear as we worked side by side.

By the time the sky turned black outside the crystal ceiling, we had alphabetized the remainder of the books and scrolls and Wynna had almost placed all of them. She said we would finish moving them in the morning and proceeded to douse the lights hanging about the expansive room. I followed her example but went in the opposite direction, meeting up with her by the door to our sleeping quarters.

"Well done, assistant," Wynna said with an appreciative smile before shoving the door open and sitting heavily on her bed.

I closed the door behind us and crossed the room to my own bed. Kicking the sandals off my feet, I slipped the new green tunic off and folded it neatly on the top of the trunk. Soft snores started to drift through the room, and I turned to discover Wynna lying on her side, still dressed in her daily tunic. I tiptoed across the stone floor and gently laid a soft, worn quilt over her, its front checkered with faded reds and yellows. The corners of my mouth twitched up in a quick smile before I slunk back to my own bed and slipped under the covers.

"Bena, where are we going?" my voice scratched out in a whisper.

"Sshh!" she hissed back at me, flapping a wrinkled hand over her shoulder.

"I've never been to this part of the Manor without Sars. I don't think we should be here," I muttered warily.

"Be quiet, will you! That's the point. You aren't supposed to be over here when he isn't around," Bena snapped. She squeezed my wrist harder even though it was already clenched in her vice-like grip.

I winced and resolved to keep my mouth shut until we reached wherever it was that she was leading me. She was much stronger than her little shriveled frame had led me to believe.

She towed me down the hallways swiftly, the soles of our soft slippers barely tapping on the tiled floors. The hallways on the west side of North Manor were more dimly lit than the others and there was a faint cloud of dust drifting through the air.

Through the windows on my left pale sunlight barely illuminated the tops of the trees that skirted the wall surrounding the manicured grounds of the Manor. The lazy sunshine reminded me it was just past dawn and I swallowed a yawn.

Bena suddenly halted her hasty shuffle in front of the unassuming door of Sars's study. She carefully turned the handle, opening the door with a faint creak. Ushering me through the crack, she closed the door and immersed us in gray shadows.

An oil lantern came to life that was resting just inside the door on a small, waist high table. The light spread through the room like soft butter on morning bread, giving the gloom some welcoming warmth.

"We must hurry and be gone before Lord Rafas returns," Bena whispered, moving towards the large table that dominated the center of the room. It was completely covered by scrolls and pamphlets, the surfaces of the pages crowded with scribbled notes and sketches.

I allowed my gaze to wander about the room for a brief moment, taking in the shelves of parchment that lined the walls on either side of the table. The familiar broad desk sat heavy and demanding in front of large crystal windows through which I could see the outline of a small fountain surrounded by greenery. Every time I had been here before the room had been impeccably tidy.

Bena stood near a corner of the desk, keeping her distance from it, and waved me over. The furniture's expanse of dark wood dwarfed the small woman even more than I could have imagined. It gave me the impression that it was an evil being, ready to pounce at any moment on our unsuspecting bodies.

"What is it, Bena? Why are we here?" I said as I crossed the room as quickly and quietly as I could.

"You need to see these," she said gravely, pointing to thick sheaves of parchment stacked and scattered on the desktop. Intrigued, I circled around behind the desk and carefully shuffled the pages to get a better look.

A name was elegantly scribed on the front of each packet, each one different than the one before. Nothing about the names stood out or seemed familiar. When I removed the cover page from the first stack, the face of a young girl stared back at me. She looked about my age and the same was true in each of the other pamphlets.

"What are these, Bena?" My voice was little more than a squeak.

"Turn the pages and you will see," she replied softly.

I followed her instructions, my hands trembling. The rest of the pages were full of notes and little diagrams. As I looked closer, I could make out simple phrases in the cramped writing like "no transformation, not enough blood, powers too weak," and "will not cooperate."

The pictures were intricate drawings of the girls in various different forms. One girl was shown covered in spotted brown fur, but her face and head were unchanged. Another was depicted with a large brown wing protruding from her right shoulder. The picture next to it showed her back crisscrossed with slashes, the one powerful wing outstretched, and a miniature skeletal version curled against her side.

"This… This girl almost looks like me when I've changed," I muttered, pointing to the images. I couldn't manage to look away. "Why is she crippled like that?" A silence spread throughout the room. I turned to Bena with questions in my eyes.

"She came to us many years ago, when I still had color in my hair. Lord Rafas thought he had found his prize, but she was not strong enough. All these girls had the certain kind of potential that my Lord wants, but none could fulfill his needs," she whispered. Bena would not look at me, or at the pages covering the flat surfaces in the room.

"What happened to them, Bena?"

Silence permeated through the room once more. I left the desk and gripped Bena's upper arms, shaking her slightly.

"What happened to them?" I repeated. Fear and anger rose in my blood to fuel my strength.

"I-I cannot be sure. At the end of each account there is a date that says, 'Disposed of.'" Her voice shook with sorrow. "Both you and I can guess what it means."

"Why didn't you try to help them, warn them?" I said, releasing her and turning my back on her.

"I did not know of these plans until a few nights ago, when I heard my Lord and Tenley discussing this. They were speaking of you," she uttered quickly.

"No, he would not treat me like that. He loves me," I said quietly though the words shrieked through my mind. I twisted the silver band around the ring finger on my left hand. "Our wedding is planned for the end of winter." I started to pace around the room slowly, my head swimming in frost-covered mud.

"The past girls did not have the strength and power he needs, don't you see? He is only using you to get more power," Bena rasped, shuffling over to me with desperation straining her face. "Please believe me. Listen to Lord Rafas and Tenley talk and then decide for yourself."

My head was pounding. There was too much to consider and too much information that contrasted what I thought I knew. I needed to get some fresh air, to get out of this darkness-infested room and into the morning light.

I nodded in response to Bena. I would listen. I would trust her for the time being and see what came of it later.

10
Unusual

WYNNA AND I FINISHED placing the new arrivals but from then on, I was tasked with memorizing how the library was organized. Hours turned into days and days became weeks. When Wynna had to run an errand for the king, she would give me the task of replacing a book on its shelf, which would usually take longer than her absence. I will never know how much of a help my presence really was, but she assured me that it was much nicer having someone to share the library with than to roam its expanse all on her own day after day.

After nearly two months of attempting to commit every book to memory, I felt the shelves and sections become more familiar and my steps that echoed through the air became surer. Pieces of my past came back to me each day, filling in voids inside me.

The king leaned over the balcony while Wynna and I took our lunch one day, yelling, "Wynna! I need you!"

"What do you require, my Lord?" she called back, rising from her seat across the table from me. She moved around one of the great book cases to stand across from him.

"I need your presence and your expertise in the royal offices, nothing more," he said, turning on his heel with a flurry. His footfalls stomped back across the second floor of the palace.

"Something has him in a tizzy," Wynna said as she came back to the table. "I should be on my way quickly. It seems as though the king's infinite patience has started to wear thin." She finished her lunch in two hasty bites and made for the double doors of the library.

"Wynna, what would you like me to do?" I asked before she could close the doors behind her.

"Why don't you research that language we found a couple months ago? We haven't had time to look at it again because of your training. Depending on what the king has in store for me, I may be gone quite a while," she replied around the doorframe, then she was gone.

I stared at the inside of the door for a moment, an unusual feeling creeping up in the back of my mind. It was not hard to guess that something was going on. Something not all that pleasant and not particularly normal. There could be any range of oddities that were unfolding in the palace. The behavior of the king was only open to speculation.

I finished my lunch immersed in silent thought and then placed the wonderful ceramic dishes by the door. Someone from the kitchens would be by soon to fetch them. I breathed in the regality of the high wood shelves and the mustiness of ancient parchment, bound and unbound alike.

This wood- and stone-filled place is beginning to feel like a new home, I thought, gazing up at the grandeur that surrounded me.

The concept curled the corners of my mouth as I weaved between the free-standing bookshelves to the enormous wall hanging. Hefting it aside, I lit the lantern that hung just inside and crossed the triangular room to the far corner. I lifted the lantern high, searching for the small leather- and wood-bound books that I needed.

As I searched, I began to wonder how I was going to move them. I most certainly didn't want to risk getting zapped again. The spines of the little books caught my eye and then I remembered the pair of soft leather gloves that Wynna kept in a little chest on one of the tables inside the Archive.

I shuffled to the table and set the lantern on its aged surface. The chest in its center was the size of a trinket box but fashioned out of heavy wood. I lifted the lid and moved aside the assorted tools to retrieve the pair of supple and wrinkled leather gloves that rested at the bottom. I shoved my hands into their comforting care and moved back to the shelf, the lantern dangling from one fist.

I risked reaching out toward the books with my empty hand. Very slowly I stretched the fingertips of the gloves toward their spines, just grazing the surface of one of the books. There was no jolt or presence of sparks. A tiny tingling sensation started in the beds of my fingernails and crept outward around my hands, but I barely noticed.

I wrapped one hand around all three books and quickly padded back toward the wall hanging. I doused the lantern, hung it in its usual place, and slipped out into the main library. I skirted the outside of the room, making my way to the shelves that hid the door to the librarian's quarters.

I tilted my head back and ran my eyes over the rows of neatly and precisely placed books in the literary section. It was narrow, only about five feet wide, but it ran from floor to ceiling. Staring at the topmost shelves, I sighed and thought, *How am I going to do this?*

I carefully placed the three little books in a stack on the floor off to the side. I crouched down, sitting on my heels, and scanned the bottom shelf, then moved up to the second, third, and so on. None of the books I saw were written in characters I recognized. After a few minutes I had to go get one of the unnervingly tall ladders in order to see any higher.

I slid it into place and shook it lightly before I cautiously climbed up ever higher in search of some familiar words or symbols. The farther I went and the more books I discarded, the more I began to think that the job might be easier than I had originally thought. The sun moved consistently across the sky overhead, shifting the shadows beneath the crystalline ceiling. My calves began to ache from retaining my balance while teetering on the ladder and from scaling the innumerable wood-plank rungs.

The edge of the windows came startlingly close above my head and my heart sank. There was only a fraction of the shelves left to search. Maybe the largest store of literary knowledge on the Continent wasn't enough.

The ache in my legs crept up my lower back and I grimaced as I stepped up to the next shelf. I didn't understand how Wynna could navigate the ladders like flat ground.

Doubt and disappointment enveloping my thoughts, I noticed something that brought back a glimmer of hope. At the far end of the shelf was a series of thick, heavy-looking volumes bound in red-brown leather. All together there were eight of them. When I reached out and slid the closest one off of the shelf, my arm dropped dramatically from its weight. I clutched the supports of the ladder, a sound of surprise escaping my lips. I would have to bring them down one by one if I planned on living until tomorrow.

My stomach did a flip when I glanced down toward the floor of the library. I jerked my head back up and focused on the book in my hand. I slowly began to descend, one agonizing step after another, concentrating on the sturdy wooden rungs beneath my feet.

My foot touched down on stone tiles and relief made my already pained even muscles weaker. After managing a few satisfying and deep breaths I looked back up to the shelf on which I had found the large books. The sight of it made dread sink in my stomach like an iron weight.

With one more deep breath and a quick stretch after setting the volume next to the other little books, I began my return up the ladder. The next book was just close enough for me to reach, and when my shaking legs were once more planted on the stone, I slid the ladder over to the right so I could retrieve the remainder of them more easily.

Up and down the ladder I continued with wave after wave of exhaustion pulsing up my legs and into my back. Bracing myself for the final trip up the ladder, I placed one foot on the bottom rung. A searing, tearing pain shot up my leg.

I doubled over, biting back a shout. A jolt of pain lashed out through my shoulders with every breath. I stumbled over to the shelves and carefully lowered myself down into a sitting position, propped up against the spines of weathered and wise volumes.

I sucked in carefully measured breaths, remaining as motionless as I could for what felt like a long time. The pain subsided to an occasional stab that accompanied any flexing of my back muscles and then finally disappeared. My mind was blank, and my body was frighteningly lethargic, reminding me of the day by the waterfall. A fleeting sense of helplessness darted through me.

The soft click of the door latch cut through the air and then wood scraped across stone. A familiar voice called out, "Nika are you here?" I eased up on to my feet and tiptoed around the shelves, careful not to aggravate any part of my body.

The breath rushed out of my lungs in relief when the doors came into view. Eith's eyes brightened to rival the moon. She rushed over and squeezed me in a much-needed embrace.

"I'm so glad to see you! Everything has been so busy for the past couple of months," she squealed.

"I know. All I've been able to think about are books. I can't imagine how it must be waiting on a princess all day," I replied. Eith's huge smile stretched across her face and she seemed to be more rested than I had ever seen her before.

"Well, I am on my toes all the time, but working in the library must be quite involved."

"Wynna certainly does have a work load, and I've only experienced part of it. Keeping all these scripts and books in line is more difficult than I expected." I gestured toward the towering shelves and scattered tables.

"I hear from Rani that Wynna has been called to the king's quarters to serve as council," Eith said, her expression becoming serious.

"I know she's there, but council for what?"

"Rani doesn't even know. All we've heard, and noticed, is that things in the palace are unusually tense and it must be something big."

"I thought the king seemed aggravated, but I haven't actually left the library since we first came here," I said uncomfortably. My work was important, but I was a little ashamed that I hadn't even tried to see the palace grounds.

"Oh my, we must amend that as soon as possible! I will speak with Rani and I'm sure she can get it sorted out," Eith exclaimed.

"Lady Eith?" a polite voice inquired from behind us. A young guard stood in the doorway. "Princess Ranalani requests you return to her quarters."

"All right, I'll only be a moment," she replied and turned her back on the guard. "Well, I suppose that's all the time I have for today, unfortunately. Rani can be very impatient sometimes," Eith added quietly, glancing toward the door. We wrapped each other in a parting embrace before heading toward the door. "Try not to work yourself too hard. Just looking at those ladders makes my knees weak."

As Eith disappeared into the hallway, I took a moment to step out of the library. What I saw up and down the corridor was completely different than the day when Malvin brought Eith and I to the palace. People and guards were bustling back and forth. Some carried papers or boxes or tools while the empty hands of others pumped at their sides as they rushed to and from various places in the palace. In the time that I stood in front of the library doors, I believe I saw the same servant pass by going in opposite directions at least three times.

There was a nervous buzz on the air like a smoke-filled breeze on a spring day. It worked its way underneath my clothes and onto my skin. Its caress was dark and crawling. I scrambled back into the library and shut the doors firmly behind me, blocking the atmosphere of the rest of the palace. I sucked cleansing breaths into my lungs, bracing both hands against the thick, solid wood, chasing the sinister air away.

I crossed the library to the place where Wynna usually stood to converse with the king. The balcony was rounded and had a waist high railing of thin stone pillars entwined by skillfully carved ivy and rose buds. They were realistic enough that they made my fingers twitch with the desire to touch their delicate petals. While I gazed up at the impressive balcony, I could not help but wonder what it was they were discussing up there in the king's offices. My eyes drifted higher to the domed ceiling where a late afternoon sun signaled suppertime. My stomach gurgled.

I jumped as one of the library doors creaked open and sighed shut with a muted bang.

"How goes the search?"

I took a deep breath and turned to face Wynna. "Oh, about as good as we should have expected," I said.

"And that means...what, exactly?" The drop of her shoulders and the dulled spark in her eyes indicated that whatever the topic was that she had discussed with the king had been taxing. She dropped onto a wooden stool and leaned an elbow against the nearby table.

"I found some volumes that seem promising, but there weren't any other books that use the same letters or symbols as our current language. I checked every title of every book in the language section," I explained.

"It is possible that books and scrolls contain information that their titles do not portray, but that is very rare, so it is likely that you have found all the information that there is." Wynna passed a hand over her face as she yawned. Worry and tension seemed to roll off of her in waves.

"Wynna, would you look at the ones I have brought down before supper arrives? Just to be sure they will actually help us," I inquired softly.

"Of course. Let's have a look!" she replied. Some light came back into her face as she stood, and we made our way toward the pile I had left next to the language shelves. She picked up one of the large books and flipped it open to a page somewhere in the middle and began to skim the paragraphs. "Weren't there eight of these?" she pondered half to herself.

"Yes, there are. I haven't gotten the rest down yet." She gave me a curious look. "They are a long way up there and I don't have nearly as much experience climbing these ladders as you."

"Ah, right, I keep forgetting that I have a distinct advantage compared to most when it comes to library work," Wynna muttered, continuing to skim through the book. "Would you get them down now please? This seems like as good a time as any."

Up the ladder I went, and then back down again. By the time I had retrieved the final volume, my leg and back muscles ached once more, but not as badly as before. Supper had also arrived, which we devoured in our little triangular room.

While we finished eating, Wynna told me that the next day she would be required to join the king again and I should begin trying to decipher the enchanted little tomes. The volumes I had found where the best source of information we were going to find in the library. If they didn't tell us anything, then the whole endeavor was sunk. Not long after we set our dishes aside, sleep swooped in for the night.

"Pain will either drive you mad or you will use it to your advantage," Lord Rafas said, his posture loose and languid as he leaned against the stone fire place. Outside my bedroom windows the forested courtyard was enveloped in darkness. A cracked moon peered in from between the branches, offering pale yellow light. "If we do not shrink from pain, it will help us realize our full potential."

"So… You mean the more frequently we change, the easier it will become?" I fiddled with loose threads on the edge of the wool blanket that covered me. I sat in a high-backed wooden chair with my toes almost in the fire. The lingering aches of illness crept across my arms and legs. A fever had

raged for days after the incident in the courtyard and the lingering weakness remained, threatening to drag me back down.

"Put simply, yes. The first is always the most difficult, and after a few months of not changing it will be much like the first time." He ran a hand across the side of his head, sweeping loose strands of hair away from his face and then fixed me with those eyes of flame. "Once you overcome the pain, you can have so much power. There are only a few of us in this world and mankind no longer knows we exist. We can have everything we have ever wanted."

I watched him carefully as he moved away from the fire and knelt before me. He fished my hands out from under the heavy blanket and clasped them between his own. What I saw in his face I could not understand. I had never seen a look like that before.

"I can give you so much more than you ever dreamed. More than the world of men can offer," he whispered, drawing something small and silver out of a pocket. "Stay with me, and I will show you the wonders of my world, our world. We can become our dreams together."

My hands flew to my mouth, which was gaping open. A week ago, I was afraid he would never want to have anything to do with me ever again, afraid that he would see me as a monster. I lifted my eyes from the beautiful silver ring to look into his face and I was lost in golden light.

11

Information

WYNNA ROSE EARLY, without a summons, and made her way to the king's quarters. She bade me to continue work on the unknown language and I shuffled into the library before the first streaks of white sunlight could stretch across the sky,

I cleared a table in the center of the library and then fetched the tiny tomes and large volumes from where I had left them the night before, the leather gloves always close at hand. I swept an indifferent hand across the dust-covered front of my deep green tunic after placing them on the table. Somehow the clothing I had been given in the palace did not fade or stain.

Bending over the leather-bound objects, I began by slipping on the gloves and opening all three of the smaller tomes to the first page. I read the strange yet simple phrase that was scrawled across the inside cover of each. It was a little odd that each phrase seemed to be written by the same hand but was not the same script as that in the rest of the books.

I set them aside but left them open and turned my attention to the first volume I had pulled from the language shelves. The stiff cover of the volume creaked as I eased it open and proceeded to slowly skim the pages. Every word I read made perfect sense and appeared to be explaining the use of the Continental Language in modern times.

Closing that volume, I moved on to the second, which was still far too familiar. The only changes were a spelling here, a meaning there, and dates going back about 100 years. By that time, it was midmorning and one of the kitchen hands brought me the usual simple breakfast of fruit, milk, and oats.

I devoured what was on my plate and took the dishes to the door.

Upon returning to my workspace, I moved the two useless volumes out of the way and began on the third, scraping some runaway kinks of yellow hair back into my long braid. The third wasn't much better than the first two and neither was the fourth. The language in each one only shifted ever so slightly.

Moving the third and fourth to join their other two counterparts, I was about to open the next volume when the doors of the library groaned open and slammed shut. I dropped the large book where I had been standing with it in my arms, adding a much smaller bang to the echoing sound of the doors.

I spun around to find a young man casually and haughtily strolling along one wall of the library. He seemed to have no concern with me, if he even knew I was there. Quickly, I stooped and lifted the volume from the floor and on to the table. I knew my duties as acting librarian and hastily made my way across the library floor to where the young man stood searching a particular shelf. As I came closer, I realized there was something vaguely familiar about him.

"Excuse me," I inquired from a respectable distance, "may I be of any assistance?"

"Not to me," he replied, giving me an uninterested glance. He pulled a book from the shelf and seemed to completely forget about my existence. He had a stiff brow and a hard mouth. An image of Kurt projected itself over his features in my mind and I frowned slightly. Why would someone so young be angry at the world, unless that was just his attitude about everything?

"In that case, I will leave you be, then," I replied curtly, turning on my heel. "Call if there is something I can assist you with."

I returned to my work, the hard, judging look he gave me hot on the back of my neck. I buried my nose in the volume I had been studying and ignored his presence, which was much harder than I cared to admit. He was quite attractive in a simple yet strong and regal sort of way. Nothing about him was exotic or unusual, which was appealing, but his manners were another story. I reached for the sixth volume and placed it in front of me, flipping open the heavy cover. One of the small tomes was snatched off the other side of the table.

"Curious words aren't they?" the young man said idly, running his hands over the book that disappeared between them. He set it back down on the table and peered at his palms for a moment before rubbing them against his dark brown pants. "What are you doing with these?" He was glaring at me as though I were not supposed to have them.

"Wynna asked me to research the language that these tomes are written in," I said, rising from my chair.

"Are you sure that's all you're doing?" he said, fixing me with silver eyes that glimmered like sunlight on a still pool. He was daring me to lie about something for which there could be no lie. When I didn't answer he said, "Why did my father send me down here with the specific purpose of keeping the new librarian's assistant company?"

"I do not know, Prince Ecco," I replied. "Perhaps he and Wynna wanted you to do just that."

"Why should a High Prince stoop low enough to keep a servant company?"

"Maybe just because the king believes it a good idea and it is a good deed."

"How do you know I am not High Prince Kol? Obviously, I could not be Prince Amr, but maybe I am the son of an influential family here in the city or of one of the Lords and Ladies of the Reaches." He narrowed his eyes at me. He was toying with me. It was a game. Despite what the prince thought, he was very easy to read.

"You are not High Prince Kol because you appear younger than he should be, and I know he has blue eyes and light brown hair. Your hair is much too dark, and you are not from one of the Reaches or another family here in the city because you have your father's eyes," I countered his condescending questions.

He studied me for a moment and said, "You have good intellect, I'll give you that, but I still do not know why my father agreed to take you on." He stepped up to me, a mere breath separating us. "Ever since you and the Liffei girl showed up, things in the palace have become increasingly unstable. We don't need you and you should not be here. My sister has acquired a great fondness for your friend, but that won't stop me from convincing my father of your uselessness."

"I like to think—"

"You don't need to think. Leave that privilege to your betters," he hissed into my face.

"—that I have more worth than you will ever be able to measure!"

A glint appeared in his eyes and I thought I saw the quirk of a grin twitch up one side of his mouth. It was only there for a moment, and then it was gone.

"I would advise you to take care with what you say and to whom you say it," he growled before sauntering out of the library with the same haughtiness he had come in with. The doors slammed behind him.

I lowered myself back into my chair, braced my elbows against the edge of the table, and put my head in my hands. My heart pounded and the hairs on the back of my neck stood on end. No one had caused me to react that way since those last few months I had lived with my father.

I leaned forward and flopped onto the big volume in front of me with a groan. The knuckles of my left hand grazed the edge of one of the tiny tomes, sending a jolt up my arm. I squealed and shot upright as one of the doors swung open again. I breathed a sigh of relief when I saw it was only Wynna.

"I figured you would be more careful with those," she teased, closing the door behind her and crossing the room to stand by my shoulder.

"I have been careful. I just had a momentary lapse in awareness due to irritation," I grumbled.

Wynna threw her head back and laughed at the domed ceiling, then slid another chair over and sat around the corner of the table from me.

"Speaking of irritation, I ran into Prince Ecco in the hallway."

"Oh no," I sighed.

"I don't think I've ever seen him in such a good mood," she said lightly.

"What do you mean a 'good mood'? If that's his good mood, then I don't want to be on the Continent when he's in a bad mood," I blurted.

Wynna laughed again. When she regained her composure, she explained the High Prince's sudden appearance.

"Nika, he was sent down here because he was being incredibly difficult and argumentative with the king. He has a frustrating personality to begin with, but lately he has been letting his intuition run wild and coming up with wild ideas about the newest personnel here in the palace."

"Yeah, I know. He granted me the esteemed privilege of his opinion of Eith and me." I fiddled with one of the wooden rods used for turning pages.

"It is not just you and Eith he is so suspicious of. There are a few new guards that began working here at the same time you did," she continued.

"Oh good, we could start a group and call it the 'Intuitively Suspicious Assembly.'"

"Nika, please," Wynna scolded. "Prince Ecco means well and has the interests of his family at heart. Unfortunately, not many people give him much credit or listen to what he has to say because he does rely on his instincts to come to conclusions."

I made an irritated noise and let the wooden rod fall to the surface of the table. I stared at the first page of the sixth volume, not actually reading but contemplating the prince. I knew what it was like to never be heard when I thought it mattered. Perhaps Ecco did have information that was true, but no solid proof.

"It is easy to tell when someone as solemn as the prince is in a good mood. He was quite pleased, and I think he likes you. I could see it all over his face," Wynna added softly. When I glanced at her there was a sly smile curving her lips. She didn't seem to be as worn out as the day before, but I did notice the dark half-moons under her eyes.

I seized my opportunity to change the subject. "Is it safe to assume that things went better today, despite Prince Ecco, since you're back rather early?"

She gave me a knowing look before replying. "The situation is still quite strange, but the king has come to the conclusion that there isn't really anything that can be done at this point. From now on we will simply evaluate any new information. Meanwhile, the king will return his attention to all the other innumerable issues in the Kingdom."

"Would it be horribly out of place to ask what the situation might be?" I managed to conceal an uncomfortable grimace. I hated to pry, but something in the back of my mind prompted me.

Wynna sighed and fiddled with the edge of one of the tiny tomes lying near her, chewing on the inside of her cheek.

"The whole palace wants to know, and everyone feels the strange, shadowy energy that permeates the halls, even though they may not all be aware of it," she said evenly. Wynna gazed at me intently and placed a hand on my arm. "Whatever is going on, I do not understand, but I do know that nothing good can come from it."

She leaned back in her chair and took a deep breath, folding her hands neatly in her lap. Staring off toward the back of the library, she announced, "Lord Sars Rafas has locked himself in North Manor and is neglecting to tend to his duties in the Northern and Eastern Reaches."

My stomach did a flip and almost jumped up my throat. A shiver of instinctual fear bounded up the base of my spine and down my arms. I wondered if I would ever be able to hear his name again without a tumult of emotions.

"I don't pretend to know anything about the duties involved with the Reaches, but I'm sure that neglecting them is not ideal for the Kingdom," I managed through my tight throat.

"No, Lord Rafas's current behavior is not good. Luckily the politics and services he has put in place over the years are solid enough to hold up during his absence. Although, I hope his condition does not carry on for too long. All great processes breakdown over time without direction." Wynna continued to stare across the library. "In a couple months crime will rise, especially with the Slavers. Traders' routes and territories will become blurred. The services for local people will fail which will lead to riots."

"You seem to know a lot about this kind of thing, Wynna," I ventured.

"About twenty-one years ago, Jiino was gripped in a brutal civil revolution. All the conditions I just listed preceded the revolution." Wynna placed her elbows on the table and turned to lock her eyes on mine. "My sister, our parents, and I fled Jiino as soon as the murmur of revolution drifted in hushed whispers down the street. The king had decided that he no longer had any interest in the affairs of his island country and went into seclusion. My father was a treasurer for the king and our family would not have fared well in the revolution. Meanwhile, all the advisors wanted to rule for themselves, since the king had no heir, and I'm sure you can imagine what a roiling mess that created."

Wynna slid one of the tomes under her nose and began to flip through it idly. There was a shrouded sadness in her eyes as she attempted to feign indifference.

"My parents took us to Linsdiil, and they still live a comfortable life there, but after a few years my sister and I wanted to see the magnificent capital of the Kingdom. We traveled a long way on our own, sticking to the well-used roads, but ended up in the city by way of Traders after taking a wrong turn," Wynna finished. "Anyway, the people of Jiino took back the throne from the warring advisors, appointed a new ruling family, and have apparently thrived ever since."

"Where is your sister now?"

"Oh, she's still here, in the city. She fell in love with the man who took us from the Traders and helps him run his business. He is twelve years older than us and they would be married by now, the heavens know he has asked her numerous times, but Daon is definitely not the marrying type. She loves independence too much." Wynna stood and went to the nearby table where I had stacked the volumes I had already searched through. She shuffled some papers and scrolls around, making more room for the linguistic work.

"Daon is your sister?" I asked as my jaw dropped.

"She is my twin," Wynna replied, turning back to me with a puzzled look.

I stared at her incredulously, and, now that I knew they were related, I could see all of the features of Wynna's face that were nearly identical to Daon's; even their figures were identical. How could I have not seen the similarities before?

"I know Daon. Malvin took me from Traders and I lived in the shop with them for a few months," I exclaimed.

Wynna gaped at me like I was a two-legged dog.

"I knew they sent people to the palace for work, but I have never met any of them, let alone have one of them sleep in the same room as me," she said softly. She shook herself and a new look appeared on her face, one I had not witnessed before, and she said, "I hope Daon wasn't too hard toward you, she has always been a rather staunch, unapproachable person."

"Oh, not at all, though I did think her a little unusual in the beginning. After a little while I understood that she is a stern, but caring woman," I replied quickly.

"Good." Wynna took a deep breath as the look of a lifetime of frustration faded from her. She glanced at the ceiling, barely a twitch of her head, and began to slowly make her way around the table in the direction of our quarters. "I don't know about you, but the setting sun is saying that I should go to sleep."

I made an affirmative noise, tidied some objects on the table and then followed my mentor to our sleeping arrangements. Wynna had left the door open and I closed it behind me.

As I crossed the room to my bed, she rustled her covers and said, "Tomorrow I won't be assisting the king, so you can show me how far you've gotten with those little books."

"I'm afraid you may be disappointed because I haven't gotten anywhere," I said, plopping down on the edge of my mattress. My sandals hit the floor with a dull clatter.

"Don't be afraid, Nika," was all Wynna had left to say for the night and I had nothing to reply.

The sun rose with an ominous red glow, haloing the spears of the trees in the west, dark sentries that guarded the backside of our town. The smell of sulfurous minerals and fires hung on the air that blew down from the north. I wrinkled my nose and hugged my threadbare shawl closer to my body. That mine would be the death of this place, no matter what the officials and merchants said.

I trudged down the excuse of a dirt road, mud sucking at my boots. The track was a cesspool waiting to be acknowledged. My bare foot squelched into the muck. I grimaced before even looking down. A few feet behind me, my half-submerged boot perkily poked out of the slime. Swearing, I pivoted on my one booted foot and yanked my other boot from the muck's grasp while keeping my balance with the bucket of water in my other hand. I would have to walk the rest of the way home with one boot on. I didn't dare put my rancid foot back in the other one.

My foot was disgusting, and my thin sock was ruined by the time the trees loomed over me. Our house was the closest to the edge of the forest to the west, and didn't warm up nearly enough to be livable, even with a fire blazing. The winter had been more awful than usual, and its icy tendrils clung possessively in the shadows of the trees.

I paused outside to wash my foot with some of the water from the bucket I carried and then went into the shack. The plank door screeched as I shut it behind me, and I placed the bucket of water just inside the doorway. Embers glowed feebly in the fire pit to my right and a groan came from the bedrolls to my left.

"Good morning, Father," I said loudly as I went to the fire pit and tossed some evergreen needles on the embers.

Another groan drifted across the hut.

"It is past dawn, and that means you should be at the mine." It was a waste of breath to inform him.

Some incoherent syllables bobbed through the air in reply.

I coaxed the fire back to life with needles from the trees and then tossed a few pieces of wood on top. I strolled across the hut to where my father lay sprawled on his stomach, retrieving the bucket of water on the way. I stood over him a moment, nudging his water skin that laid just beyond his fingertips with my toe. I tried calling to him a few more times. He didn't respond so I tipped the bucket over his head. He leaped up with a yell and I backed up against the wall to avoid getting a tooth knocked loose.

"Curse you, girl! Haven't I told you not to wake me like that?" he hollered at me after wiping the water from his eyes.

"Yes, you have, quite clearly, but how else am I supposed to rouse you when you go to sleep every night in a drunken stupor?" I yelled back at him.

He straightened to his full height and stepped in close, shoving a finger in my face and forcing me to crane my neck to look up at him.

"You know better than to speak to your father that way. I ought to teach you a lesson you won't ever *ignore," he hissed and then turned his back on me, scooping up his water skin from the floor. He didn't have the backbone to follow through on his threat and probably couldn't even think of a decent way to punish me.*

He went and stood in front of the fire and took a long drink from the leather bottle. I could smell the cheap whiskey from across the hut. Rage welled up deep inside me, just waiting to be unleashed.

"Nika?"

"Yes, Father?" I answered between clenched teeth.

"You are the most beautiful daughter a man could ever ask for and you are sixteen now, a couple months into eligibility," my father spoke to the opposite side of the room, not brave enough to face me. "By all rights I could

have cast you out a month ago and it is time that you found a husband."

"What?" I screeched in amazement. "What makes you think I want a husband?"

"I don't care what you want*! What I say is your law, and what your husband says will be your law!" he yelled, finally spinning to look at me. "You are going to have a husband in a month's time, or you are going to the Slavers!"*

He stormed over to our food box, leaving his water skin on the stool by the fire, and began rummaging through vegetables, one measly loaf of bread, and a few strips of dried and salted meat that I had bartered my tongue off to get.

Anger boiled in my gut. I tiptoed to the stool and grabbed the water skin that had never been used for water and hurried outside, not bothering to close the squeaky door behind me. A little way down the path I uncorked the skin, tipping it upside down and emptying its wretched contents.

Footsteps sounded behind me just before my father's voice boomed, "What do you think you are doing?" A moment later the world was white light and my back was pressed against the ground. When my vision cleared, I saw my father scooping his empty water skin off the ground where I must have dropped it.

My right ear stung and my eye blurred. The ringing in my ear drowned out everything. Dazed, I gingerly wiped a hand across my eye and then my ear. I blinked and squinted, my eye watering and my ear bleeding from my father's knuckles.

There was a rustle of grass and his weight settled on top of me, pinning me to the ground. The numbness in my mind from his blow dissipated, replaced by fear as his hands wrapped around my throat. He was screaming curses and threats garbled by rage.

"Fa-ther! St-stop!" I tried to plead, but his screams were too loud, and my breath was failing. My lungs burned as the last wisp of air slipped past his crushing grip. Heat seared up my back and a red haze filled my vision.

When the wall of red faded, I gasped in a searing breath. I was much farther down the path from the hut than I remembered. I looked back toward the sad building. My father was hunched over at the place where I thought I should have been. There were bright, bloody claw marks down his face. The horror that shone in his eyes wrenched my insides. He was holding his face with one hand and trying to keep his balance with the other as he staggered backwards toward the hut.

"Y-y-you're a m-monster, j-j-just like your mother!*" he sputtered and spat. I took one small step toward him and he scrambled back with a whimper. "S-st-stay away f-from me, beast!" He shuffled frantically inside and slammed the flimsy door between us. I ran to the hut and rattled the door, but he had bolted it shut.*

"Father! Father, please let me in!" I yelled, pounding on the planks. "I don't know what happened! Please, tell me what I did!"

I shrieked and beat the door until my voice was raw and my hands were full of splinters. I slumped against the wall of the building and slid to the ground. I folded my arms and legs tight against my body, the sun cold on my skin until it disappeared behind the trees. The moon rose, watery and wavering through my tears until it faded into restless dreams of clawed monsters.

12
Progress

I BOLTED UPRIGHT with a strangled cry. The dim, stone room was unfamiliar, and the stone walls were crushing in on me. Pressure swelled along my spine and my hands began to tingle.

"Nika... Nika?" a voice exploded and echoed along the walls.

I screeched and curled into a ball, covering my ears with feathered hands to douse the noise.

"Nika!"

It came again, closer, louder. Hands gripped my shoulders and rocked me back and forth.

"Nika, it's me! It's Wynna!"

Wynna... Wynna? Stone walls... The palace...the library. My panic and confusion slowly subsided. The room returned to its real shape and size, while a buzzing in my head that I hadn't consciously noticed slowly disappeared. I turned toward the owner of the hands that were still grasping my shoulders, taking in a warm, dark face. I whispered, "Wynna?"

"I'm here. You were dreaming," she said softly, eyeing my hands and arms warily.

I looked down. The backs of my hands were covered in tiny, beautiful golden feathers. My fingers were tipped by clear crystal talons. Their beauty was mesmerizing and horrifying. I thrust them away from me, my arms sheathed in the same feathers. I traced the extent of the feathers with bare fingertips up over my shoulders and around my ears.

"You should not be near me. You should run away...get away from me!" my voice rose into a shrill wail as I backed as far away from Wynna as I could. She reached toward me again and I shrieked. I pressed my arms against my chest and began to sob, staring at my terrible, beautiful talons.

"Nika, please calm down. I'm not going anywhere," Wynna said softly, sitting on the edge of my bed. "I know you won't hurt me, no matter how strange this all is."

"How do you know I won't? *I* don't know that I won't!"

"Do you want to hurt me?" she asked.

I shook my head slowly.

"Then there's your answer."

I took a deep breath and realized she was right. Everything was controlled by emotions and instincts, but I could change my emotions and curb my impulses so that everything was within my control. I closed my eyes and absorbed the safety of our room in the palace library. My fear subsided and I felt the slither of hundreds of tiny feathers retreating underneath my skin and the tickle of talons shrinking. When I opened my eyes again Wynna was gazing at me, relief clear on her face.

"There you are," she said fondly.

I gave her a wavering smile. Even though I had only woken up minutes before, my mind and body felt spent.

"Maybe you should stay in bed a little longer today. I can take care of the library by myself," Wynna offered.

"I'll be alright, just a little slow today." I waved off her suggestion. Sleep sounded infinitely appealing, but the fear of what might be lurking in its murky depths deterred my exhaustion.

"Very well, but only if you're sure..." Wynna rose from the bed and crossed to the door, turning back to fix me with a scrutinizing look.

"I'm ok, really."

She made a skeptical sound and then disappeared through the door into the library. I slumped back onto my pillow and stared at the gray ceiling. I couldn't even imagine what would happen if the king got word of what had transpired that morning. The possibility made me shiver and pinpricks danced up my spine. I rolled off of my bed, tidied the covers as best I could and then braved the expanse of the library.

Wynna stood near the table where I had left everything from the day before. She was absently flipping through one of the volumes I had already scoured.

"It seems that the information in these books is far more important than I had originally thought," she said when I emerged from between the shelves and made my way to her side. "Today will be dedicated to searching for answers. What do you think about that?" She looked at me sideways.

"That sounds wonderful," I said.

"Good, I will start with the first volume to see if I can find anything that you might have missed and you can start where you left off yesterday," Wynna instructed.

We took up positions across the table from each other. I started at the beginning of the sixth volume since I hadn't actually read any of it the night before. Within the first few pages I noticed strange words, but I could still interpret them as our own. Whenever 'the' was written it appeared as 'tah,'and 'this' was 'thiz.' As I continued, I found more simple words that were stranger than those in any of the previous volumes. When I found 'that' written as 'thet' I left my chair to go find a blank sheet of parchment.

"What are you doing?" Wynna called as I rifled through papers and scrolls across the room. I could feel her peering at me.

"Are there any blank pages around here?"

"I keep them in that wooden box by the door. Why do you need blanks? Did you find something?"

Sure enough, there was a box brimming over with blank pages tucked into a corner by the door. I grabbed a few sheets and returned to the table. As I sat back down, I handed a couple of the dry, scratchy pages to Wynna.

"Write down any words that are different from ours, just the simple ones. If I'm right, I think I can make a language key," I explained.

We continued to pour over the volumes and as I went, I realized I had been doing it the hard way. These strange words were much simpler than Wynna and I had originally believed. The seventh volume was much harder to read than the sixth and the eighth was nearly impossible, but I was practically jumping out of my seat from the amount of progress we had made. I could tell Wynna felt the same from the spark in her eyes and the excited flutter of her hands. She even had to go get more blank parchment because of the number of unusual words that we could still understand. I finished the eighth and Wynna completed her account of the fifth just minutes later.

"I think that's enough for now and we probably have enough to figure out your key," she said.

We both slumped back in our chairs just to be startled by the scrape and slam of one of the doors. Wynna and I turned in unison with curses on our lips but froze at the sight of Prince Ecco.

Dread fell upon my shoulders as Wynna greeted him cheerily. "My Lord, what a pleasant surprise. Can we help you with something?"

"Not of the ink and parchment type," he replied, fixing me with hard eyes. "I have been sent from Ranalani's chambers to carry an invitation to you." His words carried like flung daggers. It was not hard to see his displeasure at being used as a messenger boy.

"Well, this is a surprise," I said dramatically. "What might that invitation be, Prince Ecco?"

His glare deepened and I could barely contain the bark of laughter that desperately wanted to escape.

"My sister would like you to join her for a walk through the gardens this evening, 'to enjoy the sunset air' as she put it." At that point he was more uncomfortable than annoyed, no longer meeting our eyes and looking about the library instead. It would have been difficult not to notice our amusement.

"Wynna, what do you say?"

"We have done enough research for today, Nika. Besides, you haven't been outside the library since you came here," she said, gesturing for me to go.

I thanked her and followed Prince Ecco's brisk strides through the doors and up the hallway. I jogged every few steps to keep up with his clipped pace. It was as though he didn't want to allow any opportunity for conversation, no matter how brief it might be since Ranalani's rooms were just down the corridor from the library.

Prince Ecco barged through the doors to Newt Wing calling, "Rani, your package has arrived!"

His proclamation was met by eerie silence and then a door to the left swung open preceded by giggles. The princess backed through the door followed by Eith, nearly toppling Prince Ecco before he could get out of their way. Between them they carried a giant pot full of bright green fronds, sprigs of tiny orange and white flowers, and leafy plants with huge dangling purple trumpet-like blooms.

"Oh, hello brother, wonderful of you to fetch Nika for us," Ranalani exclaimed after she trampled Ecco's feet.

"What in the name of the Kingdom do you think you are doing?" The prince growled between clenched teeth as he collapsed into one of the large armchairs to nurse his injuries. I stifled a laugh that came out as a snort. The other girls did the same and Prince Ecco fixed us with one of his icy glares.

"Oh Ecco, do you have to be so *severe* all the time? Have a sense of humor for once," Rani sighed.

"Just what *are* you doing, Rani?" he asked again, ignoring his sister's retort.

"Well, Eith and I decided that since I can't spend as much time outside as I would like, we would bring part of the gardens inside," she explained.

"Oh, is that all? And what happens when you start having a reaction because you went outside without a cover?" Ecco was still rubbing his feet.

"When I start having a reaction, we'll do what we always do. Deal with it," she snapped back at him. She and Eith carefully lowered the giant planter to the floor in the middle of the room. I was still amazed that the two small-statured people could even lift the thing.

The prince rolled his eyes at his sister and grumbled, "If you were bent on doing this, why didn't you ask me to help you get the planter before I went to the library?" He stood and propped his hands loosely against his hipbones, gazing inquiringly down at Ranalani.

"I didn't ask because we always have a big discussion about the ups and downs and reasons. You always try to talk me out of everything," she replied, seeming uninterested. "Besides, I wanted you to go get Nika."

The younger girl's arms encircled me while Eith stood nearby grinning. Prince Ecco stared at me in disapproval. I winked at him and his frown deepened.

"It's so wonderful to see you again! I've tried to get Ecco to fetch you for me so many times before, but he always refused to go anywhere near the library, which was very strange because he used to spend hours in there every day. I never understood why he loved browsing those stuffy old books all the time." Rani chattered in my ear while Ecco stared at the back of her head.

"Speaking of that, I believe I will go relax in the library like I used to," he interjected, stomping to the door.

"I didn't know you could relax, my Lord," I said sweetly before he could escape into the hall. He half turned with one hand on the door, revealing that same quirk in the corner of his mouth that I had seen before, and then he was gone.

"Ah, that's much better… The one thing about Ecco that really gets on my nerves is his stubbornness. He has a bad habit of not listening, understanding, or accepting anything that differs from his ideas," Rani said, exasperated. "Lucky for me though, he usually does whatever I want with a little persuasion, but then again so does Kol." Rani shrugged with a smug grin and withdrew her gigantic umbrella from the closet. Brandishing it like a sword she said, "Shall we, ladies?"

Eith's laughter tinkled against the crystal ceiling and I said, "After you, my Lady."

Rani took us through the door she and Eith had used earlier, which lead through her washroom to glass double doors that opened into luscious gardens.

"These gardens are gorgeous." The words dribbled down my chin as the sounds of the birds in the trees and bushes enveloped me and the sweet, sultry scents wafted into my nose. We were surrounded by luscious emerald foliage and blossoms varying in color from deep midnight purple to the palest orange.

"The gardens outside End Wing are the most beautiful. That's where the fountains are," Ranalani said. She idly unfolded her umbrella and strode out into the bright foliage and scattered rainbow of flowers.

"Who lives in End Wing?" I ventured.

"That's where Ecco's rooms are. It isn't really any different than the library in there, honestly. He rarely takes visitors and mostly keeps to himself, when he isn't helping Kol with the guards and soldiers and Father with delicate situations." Rani leaned over closer to me and said more softly, "If you ever need to know anything, Ecco is the man to see, besides Wynna of course, providing you can convince him to tell you anything."

"I doubt he would even tell me the time of day," I grumbled.

"Mmm… I think you might be surprised…" Rani trailed off.

"What is that supposed to mean?" I drew my eyebrows together.

"Oh, nothing… Shall we go see the stables?" Rani deliberately changed the topic and I decided to let it go, but not before casting an inquiring look towards Eith, who just smiled.

"The stables are lovely," Eith commented enthusiastically. "I convince Rani to walk by them at least once a week."

"She has to *oooh* and *aaah* at the horses for at least half an hour before I can get her to accompany me anywhere else," Rani added.

"I've loved horses since I was little and always wanted to know how to ride." Eith got a dreamy, faraway look in her eyes.

"You never told me you don't know how to ride!" Rani whirled on her, snapping Eith out of her reverie. "I can ask Kol to teach you when he has time. I doubt you would enjoy being Amr's student." Rani leaned closer to me and said softly, "He likes to be bossy!"

"Amr is really quite charming and he's only a brat to you because you're his sister. If it's all the same to you, I would rather not spend too much time in the presence of High Prince Kol," Eith argued, glancing at me nervously. I expected anger from the princess, but instead a look of appalment spread itself across her face.

"Eith, may I speak to you for a moment?" I said lightly, taking my friend's arm. "Excuse us, your majesty."

I led Eith to the edge of the West Courtyard, just outside the princess's hearing. I grasped Eith's shoulders tightly and spun her to face me.

"What in the Kingdom is wrong with you? How could you not go to your brother when the two of you live in the palace? Why doesn't Rani know?" I hissed.

"Ow, let go! You're hurting me!"

"Eith, you need to face the past to move on with your life. You cannot hide in Newt Wing forever. When Vernier finally discovers you're here…it makes me sick to consider what his reaction might be." I loosened my grip a little. "Go to him and have the reunion the two of you deserve."

Eith lowered her face in shame and I wrapped my arms around her. I understood inner wars and how difficult they are to overcome, but I also knew what could happen when a past isn't set right.

"Oh, Nika… I've missed you these past months. I needed to speak to you so many times, but Rani had me so preoccupied… I… I suppose being a princess's attendant isn't exactly what I had expected," she told me in a small, lost voice.

She pulled back from my embrace and took a deep, shuddering breath. "I know how it looks that I haven't gone to him by now, but I haven't had the strength to do it on my own. I didn't tell Rani because she would make a big deal out of it and I want to do it on my terms."

"I agree with you, but you have never been alone," I said, taking her hands. "I am here for you no matter what, even if we aren't on the same landmass."

Her eyes grew bright and a smile to rival the sun shone on her face. She hugged me tightly and said a quiet, "Thank you."

When we returned to Princess Ranalani she was teasing a nearby guard as he assisted her in holding the umbrella. They stood near a break in the carefully placed planters that ringed the courtyard, Rani questioning him endlessly about the one that was missing from the space. She was disappointed when we interrupted her tormenting of the poor man, but also seemed to have forgotten about Eith's outburst.

As the guard scratched his head and stared at the gap in the ring of planters, we continued across the courtyard and into the trees on the other side where the flowering plants were far less abundant, and the gardens gradually came to an end. We strolled around the straight brown trunks and through faucets of sunlight, our jabbering constant until the trees gave way to a huge area of dirt and sand.

The grounds of the stables and arena were blanketed in a fine haze of dust that forever drifted on the wind. The buildings were large, square, and made of dark brown wood. They seemed rather unimpressive from a distance, but upon entering the stables I realized that every wall and post was meticulously carved with coiling vines and flowers. Where the foliage was thickest on the walls, I was startled by the friendly face of a horse carved so that it was peeking out from behind the vines and flowers.

Every carving, like every painting or tapestry within the palace, was so detailed and precise that it looked as though the plants and horses had simply decided to become part of the buildings. Far off to the left were the pale wooden walls and glass ceiling of Wash Wing, framed on either side by the edges of the trees that surrounded the stable grounds.

"Rani, why do the wings of the palace have such odd names?" I blurted as we passed the grooms' and stable hands' quarters.

"That was one of the first things I asked her," Eith said, laughter in her voice.

"The story behind that isn't nearly as exciting as one might think," Rani answered, striding across the bare dirt toward the arena. "When a new king takes the throne, he can change the names of the wings of the palace. My father didn't change the names until about five years ago, when I turned ten. He asked my brothers and I what we thought our rooms should be called. We spent days arguing about it and then Ecco and Kol, being the most educated, suggested that we base it on the compass."

"I'm not sure I understand..."

"Well, my rooms are called Newt Wing. The word 'newt' is a combination of north and west because my Wing points north-west. Likewise, Wash Wing points south-west, so 'wash' is a combination of south and west," she explained further.

"I see what you mean," I said, nodding. I peered into the distance and was greeted by the sight of high wooden posts and boards painted black wavering in the late summer heat.

When we were close enough to make out the forms of people standing around and within the enclosure, Rani exclaimed, "Oh, Amr and Kol are jumping today!" She started to jog toward the arena, Eith keeping pace under the huge umbrella. I followed close on their heels.

There were obstacles both high and low set up inside the arena. Two figures on horseback navigated their way smoothly through the course. Rani ran right up to the black boards, stuck her head through one of the gaps, and enthusiastically waved the hand that wasn't holding her umbrella. The taller of the two riders noticed her instantly and called to the other before trotting our way.

"Hello ladies, how goes the afternoon stroll?" Prince Kol smiled warmly down at us for a moment before he dismounted and ducked through one of the spaces between the boards.

"It's just lovely! You know about my wonderful attendant, Eith, and our Assistant Librarian, Nika," Rani introduced us.

"It is very nice to see you again, Eith, and I've heard quite a lot about you, Nika," Prince Kol said, taking our hands in turn. I glanced at Eith. The look on her face worried me that she might faint.

"I would like to introduce you to a very good friend of mine," Kol said to Eith alone. Every time he looked at her, it was as though Rani and I weren't there.

He waved someone over from the other side of the arena. The dark hair and sturdy bearing of Vernier Liffei came into view. Eith saw too and I grabbed her hand tightly to prevent her from running away. Vernier halted before his sister, the pain and confusion plain on his face was reflected in the tears that slid down Eith's cheeks.

Vernier turned to Prince Kol, his voice haunted as he said, "Excuse us, your highness." He reached out, gently took Eith's hand from mine, and led her away from the arena.

The two royal children stared after them with shocked expressions, but I just smiled. A commotion came from inside the arena and I turned to see Prince Amr lying on the ground cradling his left arm. A group of guards were trying to calm his frenzied horse. My skin began to crawl. There was a lone guard stalking toward the boy from the fringes of the arena. As he drew closer, he put a hand on the sword at his hip. Danger spiked up my spine. I slipped through the boards and sprinted at the guard. He drew his sword, lifting it high. I screamed, knowing I was too far away to help.

Then the guard was sprawled on the ground, his sword laying yards away. I stood between him and the young prince. My breath came in gasps as I checked myself, searching for any sign of my secret. There was no way I could have closed the distance to Amr before the guard struck, but there I stood, and the boy was unharmed.

"Are you alright?" a voice said in my ear. Someone grasped my arm, my body jolting in response. I saw that it was only Kol and nodded.

A few guards were restraining the man who had threatened Amr's life. As they walked past, he glared at me with eyes that faded from glowing gold to brown. My heart wrenched as though I had been stabbed with a thick blade. I fell to my knees when the man was no longer watching, gulping air as a strange buzzing filled my ears.

"Nika? Did you know that man?"

I looked up into Kol's shimmering blue eyes and managed to forget about gold. "No, he reminded me of someone I used to know," I said, climbing back to my feet. The arena was empty around us. Amr had already been taken away.

"He is going to the infirmary, but he should be fine, just a little shaken," Kol told me, reading my expression. "I'm not sure how you did it, but you saved his life. For that, our family is indebted to you."

"I…I should go back to the library," I muttered and made my way to where Rani stood on the other side of the railing, shakily hefting the enormous umbrella on her own. I took one of the handles from her and we walked back to her rooms. The look on her face told me that Kol had ordered her to stay out of the arena, and she was not happy about it.

The door slammed behind us and rattled the innumerable windows of Newt Wing. I nearly jumped out of my skin and whirled to face Rani. The space was empty where she should have been and a moment later, I heard more doors opening and closing. I turned and crossed Rani's washroom to peer through the cracked door to her receiving room.

Rani was rummaging through her closet. She stood upright with a frustrated sound, her shoulders rigid. She flung the waiting umbrella from the floor where she had dropped it into the closet and slammed the door shut.

"Nika!" she yelled. I knew she wasn't angry at me, but she was thoroughly flustered.

"I'm here," I replied softly, stepping into the room.

"Oh good," she sighed. "I thought you might have left already. Would you ask Wynna to get Amr's old blanket? I used to have it here, but I just remembered moving it to a closet underneath the staircases. I am going to the infirmary, and if Father isn't there, I'm going to find him."

Then the princess was gone, and I was left alone in her chambers with an unspoken answer poised on my tongue. I sighed and left Newt Wing, heading back to the library.

I didn't know how I reached Prince Amr in time or why I had noticed the deranged guard while everyone else had been oblivious. Most of all I couldn't understand why the guard had eyes that resembled Lord Rafas's one moment and eyes of his own the next. Something was nagging at the back of my mind, but I couldn't quite grasp it.

As I stepped into the library, I called out for Wynna. When she appeared, I told her what had happened and relayed the princess's request. Shock and worry made creases around her mouth. I told her about how I had prevented Prince Amr from being harmed. Surprise sparked in her eyes and she laid a calming hand on my shoulder before rushing out of the library.

I stifled the lanterns around the library and then drug myself to our chambers. I sunk heavily onto my bed. I wondered if anyone had seen the guard's strange eyes or noticed the impossibility of my movements. As I sat alone in the dim, stone room my thoughts began to run away from reason and became a playground of unrest.

How did I know that I could even trust Wynna? There wasn't anyone that I knew would not whisper to the king that he was housing a monster.

My skin began to prickle, pressure building along my spine and at the base of my skull. I needed open air. I needed to see the sky and feel the breeze.

Words buzzed through my mind. *Your secrets are not safe You will never be safe. Come home… Return to me.*

I gasped for breath, air refusing to move in or out of my lungs and bolted from the small room into the darkness of the library. I spun circles, not seeing, and cried to the ceiling, "Never! Get out of my head!"

I stifled an angry screech with both hands while the tiny golden feathers emerged along my skin. I stared at my hands. Footsteps echoed in the hallway and I choked off a sob. I ran to the back of the library and hid behind the door to the sleeping quarters.

Wynna stopped dead in her tracks when she saw me peeking at her. I sighed in relief and came out from behind the door while the feathers disappeared, along with the incessant buzzing.

"How is he?" I blurted.

"There was no harm done except a broken wrist. Prince Amr is well and awake and harassing all those who come near him," Wynna informed me, "which is nothing out of the ordinary."

She wrapped an arm around my shoulders and led me into our quarters, making me sit down on my mattress again. Wynna lowered herself down beside me and we endured a few minutes of silence.

"I will never tell anyone about you as long as I live, unless you request it," she said finally.

I turned and met her steady gaze. At that moment I knew I was safe, from her at least.

"Thank you," I said softly.

"Some explanations would be nice though." Wynna stood and crossed the small room to her own bed. "When you are able to give them," she added with a tiny smile as she laid herself down.

"You will be the first to have them," I replied quietly, smothering the lantern and letting night take its place.

"Where in the Kingdom did my knife go?" Bena stood with her fists on her hips as she scrutinized the countertops of the kitchen.

I held back a giggle and glanced sideways at Sars, who was trying not to grin. I could clearly see the knife directly in front of Bena. She turned to scan the rest of the kitchen, confusion turning the corners of her mouth into a frown. When she turned back to the cutting board where she had been working on a soup for dinner later that night, her hand shot out and grasped the knife by the handle.

"Hah! There you are! Thought you could hide from me, eh?" she exclaimed as she returned to decapitating a carrot.

"See? It's simple," Sars murmured in my ear.

We were sitting quietly at the corner of the main island in the middle of the kitchen, well outside earshot of Bena if we whispered.

"Now you try," he nudged me with an elbow.

"You haven't even explained how to do it yet," I reminded him.

Tenley entered the kitchen from behind us and gave me a sneer as he passed on my left. He helped himself to the remaining hotcakes Bena had made for breakfast.

"Good morning, my Lord," he said, haughty as ever. "Miss Fobess."

I stuck out my tongue at his back, prompting Sars to scold, "Be nice."

"Try telling him that," I retorted. He gave me a look meant to remind me that I was considered above Tenley in nature's scheme.

"Alright, start by seeing what Tenley is seeing." I knew exactly what he was seeing: breakfast, and probably making rude comments to himself about me at the same time. "Then imagine what you would like to see and superimpose that picture over the top of what is real."

I pushed my aggravation aside and imagined a baby grass snake slithering across the counter toward Tenley's plate. Tenley jumped in the air and swatted at the empty counter. He seemed to think he had swept the snake onto the floor, so I played along. The imaginary snake slithered across the floor and Tenley chased it with a broom, under the kitchen doors into the parlor, and from there out to the main hall where it disappeared.

Tenley followed it all the way until it disappeared. When he reentered the kitchen Sars turned to him with concern and said, "What was that?"

"A snake tried to climb its way into my breakfast. I swept it all the way out to the main hall, but it disappeared. Everyone should keep an eye out for it," Tenley replied. He shoved the broom back into its corner, inhaled his food, and briskly exited.

"Well, aren't you just full of surprises. That was quite impressive for a first try." Sars stood and offered me his hand.

"Thank you. That was much simpler than I had thought it would be." I took his hand and slid down from the stool. He led me out of the kitchen into the main hall.

"For a first time it should not have been that easy," he said half under his breath.

Sars stopped just inside the main hall. He took both my hands in his and looked down at me, his eyes alight with wonder and curiosity.

"There is something remarkable about you, my love. More so than I had realized that night of the garden incident."

I stood transfixed as I gazed into the hypnotic warmth of his eyes.

He stepped in close and bent his head to whisper in my ear, "Show me something."

I glanced down at our clasped hands, the ring on my left hand catching my eye. I had never even held hands with a man affectionately before. Standing there with Sars, so close, my mind pictured what it might be like to be kissed. The thought morphed into an image of Sars lifting my chin and…

His lips pressed against mine. The touch shocked me back into the real world, snapping the connection. We each took a stiff step back. I stared at Sars, my eyes wide. I had just forced a lord to kiss me. It may have been unintentional, but it could still have serious consequences.

"I'm so sor—" I said hastily.

He placed a finger lightly over my lips and a chill ran down my back. I drew in a sliver of breath. His eyes shone with pleasure.

"That is called Pirzuezian. *Our tricks in the kitchen are* Iluzian. Pirzuezian *is much more difficult to successfully induce," he said. "I'm afraid I have work to do today, love. I will see you again at supper."*

He bowed to me and headed toward his wing of the manor. The rigidness of his spine indicated that he was struggling not to hurry.

13
Revelation

THE MORNING STARTED EARLY with a grizzled and gray guard in fancy armor pounding on the door to our little room. I sat bolt upright while Wynna groaned and buried her face in her pillow. The pounding ceased for a couple minutes and she seemed to go back to sleep. When it started again, she pushed herself into a semi-upright position.

"Would you mind doing the honors?" she grumbled across the room to me.

I nodded and swung my feet to the chilled floor. I paused to shove on my cloth slippers before padding to the door.

"Oh good. I was about to kick the door down," the guard said, his face as unreadable as stone. "Are you Miss Nika Fobess?"

"Yes, what can I do for you?" I rubbed one eye and peered at him through the other. He was much older than any of the guards I had seen posted around the palace grounds and the detailing on his uniform was much more intricate. The flick of his gaze told me Wynna had appeared in the doorway behind me.

"King Prentivus has requested to speak with you in the throne room," he replied. "He is awaiting your presence."

I turned to Wynna. She looked bewildered and groggy but shrugged and motioned for me to go. I could tell she was concerned but really wanted to go back to sleep.

I took a moment to shrug a tunic on over my nightclothes before I closed the door behind me and followed the guard out of the library. The halls were deserted, though voices purred behind doors and the sound of clattering dishes came from the kitchens when we passed. Lanterns still lit the corridors, casting flickering shadows along the walls. When we entered the throne room, I looked up through the glass ceiling. The sun hadn't even begun to rise.

"Ah, Nika, how wonderful of you to join us," Prentivus called to me as we approached.

Both High Princes and the jittery man with glasses were watching our approach intently. The king was following my movements with a warm smile that made me a little more comfortable. I stopped before the steps that led up to the tree where King Prentivus sat, my back to the giant map of the Continent and Jiino. My escort moved forward to stand by the man with glasses. They appeared to be about the same age.

"Thank you for fetching her, Captain," Prentivus addressed the guard.

The captain bowed his head to the king. He must have been the Captain of the Guard.

"Miss Fobess," the king turned back to me, "I called you here because I would like to hear your version of the events that took place yesterday afternoon."

I stared at the king for a moment. His bluntness surprised me, but I should have expected it. He was the king after all and didn't have time to chat all day.

Gathering my thoughts, I relayed my experience to Prentivus and the present company. I started with the walk through the garden with Eith and Rani and ended when Rani and I returned to Newt Wing. I left out my observation about the guard and that I wasn't sure how I had reached Amr in time.

"Something isn't right," Ecco burst out when I finished. "Why did you notice the commotion inside the arena?" There was a glint in his eye that made my stomach clench.

"Ecco, relax," Kol said softly to his brother.

"Why did you see the guard and no one else did?" Prince Ecco's suspicion beat against me in waves.

The Captain cleared his throat and the king shifted in his seat.

"I don't know…" I said quietly, but the prince wasn't listening.

"No one understands exactly what happened. All of the stories are filled with holes. There is something you aren't telling us, and I aim to find out what it is," Ecco continued. He took a step in my direction. I was afraid that the eyes of the man wearing glasses would pop out of his head.

"Ecco, that is enough!" the king snapped, a wave of energy pulsing through the air.

I blinked hard, trying to clear my head. Ecco and Kol did the same.

"Captain, please escort Miss Fobess back to the library." The king spoke calmly but there was irritation festering behind his reasonable façade.

The captain stepped forward and led me out of the throne room. Before the doors could shut behind us, I heard King Prentivus raise his voice in angry tones. The same energy that I had felt was probably rocking the minds of Ecco and Kol. I wasn't the only one in the palace with secrets, but I wasn't bent on delving into people's business.

"Wynna, I swear Prince Ecco doesn't like me at all," I said after explaining to her what the king had wanted.

"Nika, the only thing Prince Ecco has ever disliked is change. Unfortunately for you, change has come to the very air of the palace at nearly the same time of your arrival," she replied calmly.

"He doesn't verbally attack Eith." I pouted, staring at the page of strange words that lay on the table between my elbows.

Wynna sighed and put down her writing charcoal. She fixed me with a serious gaze. "I didn't want to tell you this, but it is not difficult to see that there is something different about you. I told you before: Ecco is an extremely intuitive person. If anyone here in the palace was ever going to find out about your secret it would be him."

"What about the king?" I asked softly.

"What about him?"

"There is something different about him as well, something familiar."

"Every descendant of the Lucan bloodline has had a certain unexplainable quality about them. All successors have been different than their predecessor. None of them have ever been cruel and that is why they are the only family to have ever ruled the Kingdom. Although some have certainly been more ambitious than others."

"I did not know that. Does everyone in the city know?"

"Everyone in the capital and within all the cities. When I lived in the Southern Reach everyone talked about it like old news. I cannot speak for anywhere else, but the Northern Reach is much more isolated than the others."

"I definitely know about that. I was so isolated the silence sounded like screaming."

"Are you just going to contemplate the prince and the royal family like you're love struck, or actually get somewhere with this research today?" Wynna teased, narrowing her eyes at me.

"What? Of course, I am." I sat up as straight as the edge of a sword and grabbed the sheet of words off the table. "I am not love struck in any way."

"Fine, if you say so. You may want to rethink Ecco's apparent dislike though."

"That is *not* going to happen unless he starts being civil," I declared, focusing all of my attention on the paper between my hands.

Wynna laughed softly from across the table but said nothing else.

Hours of staring at strangely familiar words had my brain crisscrossed before the sun stared down at us through the crystal. Wynna made me replace books on the shelves for a while after our midday meal because she was afraid my eyes might jump out of my head and run away. When there was nothing left to shelve, she let me return to deciphering.

I knew simple words like 'the' and 'that' were *thi* and *thet* in the old language, but then there were words that seemed to have no translation whatsoever. Groaning, I banged my head on the table in front of me and closed my eyes. What else was there that could help me? What did I know but could not remember?

I lifted my head and propped my chin on the table. A word caught my eye on one of the other pages that I hadn't looked at yet. I slid it across the table slowly and peered at the word: *Pirzuezian*. A door opened in my mind and I instantly knew what it meant. Another word came to me from the dream I had the night before: *Iluzian*. I shuffled through the sheets of parchment until I found a blank page and scratched down what had come to me.

I scanned over the pages again, finding the shortest, simplest words. Some of them were still nonsense, but others gave me more insight. One word was *zald,* and I knew it had to start with S, which led me to think that the only word I knew that was similar to that was 'sold.' After a few more hours of brain wrenching, my list was more complete, but still nowhere close to finished. Without the more complicated translations we still couldn't get anywhere:

O TO A

A TO E

E TO I

C TO S

S TO Z

DOUBLE CONSONANTS TO SINGLE

DOUBLE VOWELS STAY DOUBLE

"Wynna!" I called, clutching the partial key and shoving my chair back.

"What is it?" her voice floated down from above. I spun in a circle, my neck craned back to see the tops of the shelves. She stood as though floating on one of the ladders with a stack of leaflets on her arm.

"I've managed to figure out the simpler part and wrote it down so that our language can be translated into the old one," I explained.

"Wonderful! What do you think about a break?" She started walking down the ladder, deftly slipping leaflets onto the selves as she went. No matter how many times I saw her do that, I still could never believe it. My mouth hung open as I stared, and my stomach did a flip flop for her.

We strolled side by side down the corridors of the palace. I had no idea where we were going, but Wynna seemed to have a destination in mind. After minutes of walking down a massive, straight corridor we passed adjoining hallways that ran at angles from the corridor that we were following.

"Those lead to the throne room," Wynna said in my ear, startling me.

I turned quickly to look at her, a question in my eyes. The adjoining hallways were stone. I remembered them from when Eith and I had been introduced to the king. The main corridors of the palace were all exquisitely worked wood, not stone.

"The throne room and the parts of the palace that are directly connected to it are very old. Everything made of wood was built much later," she explained simply.

"Our quarters and the library are stone," I added.

"Yes, the library, the throne room, and parts of the upper level are ancient."

"How ancient?"

"They are older than the origin of the Kingdom."

"How is that possible? Who would have built it?" I exclaimed.

"Those records are yet to be found, if they even exist." Wynna's tone and the look on her face told me that the conversation was over. She could not give me the answers to the questions I asked and that pained her.

We came to the end of the hall and turned right to another corridor that was identical to the one we had just left. We paused in front of double doors that were much like the doors of the library. There were carvings of peculiarly shaped phials and bottles intertwined with the vines that rambled across their surface.

I opened my mouth to ask where we were, but Wynna turned to face me and said, "This is the Royal Hospital. I thought you might like to visit Prince Amr and see for yourself that he is recovering well."

"Of course, but it isn't necessary," I replied.

"Nika, you will go crazy if you stare at those books any longer and this will be good for you. Besides, I feel bad that you've been here all summer and practically never left the library."

She pushed her whole weight against one of the giant doors. It groaned as we entered and about fifteen men and women turned towards us with mild interest but then returned to their work. Beds lined the walls of the infirmary and two rows ran down the center, the beds placed head to head.

"This way." Wynna linked her arm with mine and led me all the way to the back. As we approached the rear wall, laughter came from behind one giant white curtain.

"Wynna! I was wondering when you wouldn't be able to resist seeing me again, even in my incapacitated state," a young male voice rang out as Wynna slipped through the curtain.

"I don't believe I would ever classify you as 'incapacitated,' my Lord," she replied with a curtsy. I entered behind her.

"Who is this lovely creature that you've brought with you?" Prince Amr inquired, looking me up and down in such a manner that made me blush.

His smile was a mirror image of his father's, though with fewer laugh lines and more flirtation. Deep brown eyes shone through droopy tufts of reddish hair. I imagined that Amr looked exactly like Prentivus did when he was thirteen, except for the differences in hair and eye color.

"I am Nika Fobess, your Highness," I said, curtsying the same way Wynna had.

"My mysterious savior, and Ecco's notorious torment. It is a pleasure to make your acquaintance finally and I must thank you for saving my life."

"It is wonderful of you to come visit him in here." Rani's voice startled me from across the room. She sat in a darkened corner with Eith by her side, sheltered from the sunlight that came in through the clear glass of the roof. Eith had a smile plastered to her face the likes of which I had never seen there before.

"We needed a break from the work in the library and I thought it would be a good idea for Nika to visit Amr instead of always asking me how he's fairing," Wynna said slyly, winking at me.

"You've been desperately inquiring about my welfare, have you?" Amr smiled broadly. He fixed me with his dark eyes that shimmered with mischief as well as something else I couldn't describe. "Well then, if Ecco ever gives you a hard time again, let me know and I'll give him a taste of his own medicine."

The young prince sat up straighter and tipped his chin toward the high ceiling. Out of the corner of my eye I could see Eith covering a laugh with her hand while Rani just shook her head and smiled.

"Ecco and Amr are always after each other about something. I think it's because Amr reminds Ecco of how he was seven years ago," Rani said.

"Are you serious?" I asked, incapable of keeping the shock from my face.

"Of course. Ecco was a terrible tease and had all the girls in the palace worshipping the ground he walked on. He was a nuisance to the rest of us, even worse than Amr," she explained.

"Rani, come on, you're ruining my reputation!" Amr scowled at his sister. She just crinkled her nose and stuck out her tongue at him.

"After Ecco turned sixteen, he started to rely on his intellect for everything and became suspicious and bitter," Rani sighed. "It didn't help that Father assigned him to assist Kol with our security and military as Head of Information."

"What do you mean 'Head of Information'?" I asked as I helped Wynna pull a couple chairs to the edge of Amr's bed.

"It means he is supposed to keep tabs on all suspicious activity related to the Kingdom's security," Amr answered. "He even has his own team of guards." The young prince appeared to be pouting. Apparently, he thought it would be great to have his own team to order around.

"Kol directs the movements of the troops throughout the Kingdom, under Father's approval, and Ecco gathers information to make Father's and Kol's decisions easier. At least that's the point. Sometimes the information doesn't make anything easier," Rani continued.

"So that's why Ecco and Kol are rarely at the palace at the same time," Eith piped up.

"Sadly, yes," Rani sighed again, "and when they are, it is to hold council with Father and plan the next move."

The room fell silent and then Wynna said softly, "There are thousands of people who envy royalty, but the royals would never wish their duties on others."

Rani and Amr nodded their heads.

"At the other end of the spectrum, there are those who would gladly take the duties of royalty over what life had given them, no matter the sacrifices," I added.

Wynna and Eith looked at me with understanding in their eyes. No matter where you went, one situation wasn't really ever that much better than another.

"Will someone please tell me how this conversation got so depressing?" Amr cracked the quietness in the room. "I was hoping we would be making fun of Ecco by now."

"How were you planning on slandering me to these ladies, Amr?" Ecco inquired from where he leaned against the wall by the curtain. No one had heard him come in and we all jumped at the sound of his voice.

The hairs on the back of my neck bristled and my gaze hardened as he examined those gathered around Amr's bedside. Energy snapped underneath my skin when his eyes settled on me. Wynna tensed and I knew she felt my barely contained irritation.

"Nika and I were just about to go back to the library for the evening," Wynna said, rising from her seat and gesturing for me to follow her. "May I offer you my chair, Prince Ecco?"

"No, thank you, Wynna. I was actually hoping Miss Fobess would do me the honor of accompanying me for a walk," he said eloquently, turning and giving a bow in my direction.

My jaw nearly dropped to the floor. He extended a hand and suspicion crept into the recesses of my mind as his eyes almost begged me to say yes.

"I suppose if the High Prince wishes it. Wynna, what do you say?" I replied hesitantly, not wanting the decision to be entirely my own.

"If the High Prince wishes it," she echoed my words.

I shot her a glare that said, *You're helpful.*

"But do *you* wish it, Miss Fobess?" Ecco tried again.

I paused, weighing my words. "I do not wish it, but I will indulge my curiosity of what it is you may have to say." Out of the corner of my eye I saw Rani and Eith's shocked faces, though both Wynna and Amr were grinning wickedly.

"Very well, shall we?" Ecco offered an elbow.

I stared at his arm until uneasiness wafted off of him like smoke. Only then did I turn and start walking toward the doors of the Royal Hospital.

14
Amends

PRINCE ECCO FOLLOWED AFTER ME, the sound of his boots on the floor tapping along behind me. When I glanced over my shoulder, he had shoved his hands into his pockets. There was something comical about the image that reminded me of someone who had been scolded. I turned to face him as the door swung closed at his back.

"Do you really want to walk with me, or just ask infuriating questions again?" I spat at him.

He ignored my outburst and continued walking down the hall. The tiny hairs on my body seemed to sizzle. I clamped down on my frustration before it brought out the other part of me that I most definitely did not want the prince to see.

I followed him down the corridor in the opposite direction from which Wynna and I had come. At the end of the corridor were more double doors engraved with wild horses rearing and galloping across their surface. We passed the doors, turning right to the expanse of another long and wide hallway.

"Those were the doors to Amr's rooms and up ahead we'll pass the kitchens and alchemy lab," Ecco said drily, as if giving a tour of the palace.

I clenched my jaw and made a noncommittal sound.

Ecco stopped abruptly. I bumped into him and immediately recoiled. The skin of my shoulder sizzled underneath my tunic where I had touched him. He started talking quickly, but I didn't hear a word. I stared up at him thinking, *The royal family gets more and more unusual each time I encounter any of them.*

"Miss Fobess?"

"Hm? Oh, sorry. What were you saying?" I mentally shook myself and refocused on the prince.

He let out a long sigh and glowered at me for a moment. "It has come to my attention that my behavior towards you has not been...appropriate and certainly not warranted."

"Oh, is that all? From what I can tell, you're on some sort of warpath to drive people away, but if that were the case then you would have to humiliate and degrade more than one person." My frustration erupted and Ecco looked like I had slapped him.

I stomped past him, trying to appease my nerves by moving. He grabbed my wrist and spun me to face him again. My skin sizzled and he dropped my hand abruptly, glancing at his own for a moment.

"I'm trying to apologize for my actions towards you. I never should have said any of those things," he said softly, gray eyes pleading.

"I get the feeling that you say all kinds of things that you know you shouldn't," I countered.

"I believe that makes two of us," he snapped back. "You say things to me that no one else would dare."

"Don't you forget it."

We glared at each other for what seemed like ages. I sensed the few servants that passed giving us inquiring looks. Eventually, the prince straightened his shoulders and looked as though he was accepting a defeat.

"Can we just agree to disagree and leave it at that?" He rubbed his forehead and then squeezed the bridge of his nose.

"Can you be civil and treat me like an actual person?"

"What does it look like I'm doing right now? I'm trying to apologize for saying the wrong things and all you can do is make me feel even more like an idiot. Have you even listened to anything I've said?"

I folded my arms over my chest and narrowed my eyes, studying him closely. The thought occurred to me that the prince's features were quite appealing when he was upset. The rigidness with which he always held himself had fallen away.

The first time we had met flashed in my mind. He hadn't listened to anything I had said. "Apparently we are more alike than either of us thought," I replied softly.

He sighed, extending a hand. "Truce?"

I contemplated his fingers like they were venomous snakes before grasping his hand. "Fine. Maybe next time you'll get to know someone before laying blame or judgment."

I turned on my heel and plodded up the corridor toward where he indicated the alchemy lab would be. His footsteps sounded springy beside me. I glanced sideways at him and there was the hint of a smile quirking the corners of his mouth. I was appalled to find the creases around his lips attractive. He regarded me with a peculiar look in those sparkling gray eyes. It was almost as though he were searching for the missing piece to a puzzle.

"What?" I said exasperatedly.

"Hm? Oh, nothing," he replied hastily. The look on his face disappeared and he looked straight ahead. It was my turn to stop in the middle of the hallway.

"I doubt High Prince Ecco ever gets a look like *that* over *nothing*."

"I just...there is something so peculiar about you...different."

I fought back a nervous gulp as the base of my spine tingled in warning. "What do you mean?"

"I can't really explain it, just like I can't explain how I know where to get important information from people I've never met," Ecco muttered at the floor. He ran a hand through his dark hair. I had to take half a step closer to hear what he said next. "It's a feeling that makes me bristle with the possibility of danger, but at other times it makes me extremely drawn to you."

My mouth fell open before I could stop it. The prince glanced sideways at me and turned a deeper shade of pink. I snapped my jaw shut and gathered myself. "This conversation seems rather childish for a prince of twenty, don't you think?" I said softly.

"I've seen people twice our age act equally as childish when it comes to these types of conversations," he countered without missing a beat. That sneaky, stubborn smile toyed at his lips again.

"And just what type of conversation might this be, Your Highness?" I slipped my arm through his and started walking again. Some of the stiffness eased out of his muscles underneath my hand.

"I suppose we'll have to find out."

"I suppose so," I said, smiling up at him. A spark lit up behind his eyes and I secretly celebrated the achievement of breaking Prince Ecco's façade. "But first you might try being nice to me because I don't think I like you quite yet."

He leaned in close as a few people passed us, his breath tickling my ear. "And I have yet to decide whether it's a good idea to let you stay in the palace."

I let my arm drop and clenched my jaw, picking up my pace.

"Nika, wait!" he called after me. A moment later my wrists were held in a very strong grip. I nearly stepped on his feet when he grabbed my arms, which brought us into uncomfortably close proximity.

I stared up into his silver eyes and forgot my agitation for a moment. My thoughts were of moonlight on water and the unexplainable sorrow that shone in his face. He looked like a statue come to life when he cleared his throat and tucked his hands behind his back.

"Nika, all I mean is that I know you are hiding something of great weight, and I can't stop thinking about it," he explained softly, avoiding my gaze. "Thinking about you."

Fear made me desperate and my words harsh as I struggled to suppress the panic rising inside me. "Rani was right, you rely on intellect for information that may or may not be true. Maybe you should go help Prince Kol instead of worrying your intuition over me." I spun on my heel, my pace clipped as I made my way back to the library.

I gulped down air as I sagged against the inside of the library doors. I could sense that Ecco was still motionless in the hallway where I had left him. He slowly turned and disappeared through a door to the evening outside, his sorrow growing deeper. My heart twisted. Ecco had tried to be kind and I had spat it back in his face, but I could not risk discovery. I focused on steadying my breathing, starting to convince my instincts that any threat was gone.

"Nika?" Wynna's voice came from close by in the dark.

My heart rate spiked again, and I groaned in response, squeezing my eyes shut.

"What is it? Why are you like this?" she added.

I opened my eyes again and found her standing in her nightclothes.

"Oh, my," she exclaimed, placing a hand over her mouth.

"What?" I glanced over my arms and hands for any sign of the dreaded feathers and talons. I looked back up at Wynna and realized I could see every feature of her face as though she was illuminated by white light. "Is the moon really that bright tonight?"

"No, it isn't. Nika, your eyes are glowing bright green, like a cat in the dark," she said.

I ran to our quarters. I flipped open the lid of Wynna's trunk and pulled out her little square mirror. Just like she said, my eyes glowed back at me. A scream rose in my throat, but I clamped down on the rising emotions within me. I took a deep breath and turned at the sound of rustling fabric.

"I have to know what I am, Wynna, and those books are my best chance," I said to her as she clutched the door frame.

"In that case, we will begin at first light again tomorrow," she replied softly.

"If anyone else discovers me and knows you gave me aid, you could be severely punished. I don't want that to happen."

"You have my help whether you want it or not," she said, moving away from the doorway. She placed her hands on my shoulders. "I have lived a long and full life. I do not fear what others may believe or what action they may choose to take."

Stubborn resolve lined her face, daring me to try and sway her. All I could do was whisper, "Thank you," and then she ordered me into bed.

"History is a subject that is often underestimated… Don't you think?" Sars twirled his feathered quill between his fingers as he watched me from across the room. As he spoke, I brushed my fingertips over the strange titles that lined the shelves of his study.

"Empires and kingdoms certainly rise and fall despite it," I replied. "I'm afraid I know nothing of history other than that there is always a beginning to everything."

"Hmm…" He made a quizzical sound and stood abruptly.

I turned to face him as he strode towards me. His eyes never failed to stun me.

"I believe it is time for a history lesson." A grin quirked the side of his mouth as he took my hand and led me to a small bookcase with clear crystal doors. He opened the doors and removed a plain brown tome of moderate size. Its cover was clean, supple leather.

"This book is very important to our history and that of the Continent." He grasped it between his hands as we walked to the table in the center of the room.

"It doesn't look very impressive," I said, mostly to myself.

"Never allow looks to deceive you, my dear. This is the only surviving copy of the information inside, and I am very fortunate to have acquired it."

"You seem to have quite a few volumes like that around here," I observed, referring to the peculiar designs and names that lined his walls.

"Yes, well, I have a few," he replied quietly, pride lilting in his voice. "Anyway, this one recites the ancient history of the Continent as well as the palace."

"What is so important about the palace?"

"The palace proves to be everything, love." A spark lit up in his face and he briefly caressed my hand where it lay on the surface of the table before continuing. "Unfortunately, this book is written in the old language, so it would be impossible for you to read it yourself. I will have to translate it for you, at least the most essential parts."

"Alright, I don't see how that would be a problem."

"Very well. For the time being I will give you the condensed version on account of the fading light and the imminence of supper," he said lightly. The fountain outside the windows of his study had fallen into shadow, though its trickling sounds still filled the air between our words.

I laughed as he nudged me with his shoulder. He opened the book and flipped through the pages, stopping every once in a while, on ones that were apparently vital to my history lesson.

"Long before humans came to the Continent, the lands were kept by an old and powerful species. They called themselves the Lyukians and were made up of four different races: Kylth, Mawyl, Lykke, and Iryl. Even though each race was very different from the others, they used their similarities to forge an unbreakable alliance, which was not even swayed by the invasion of man.

"The Lyukian Temple in the center of the Continent was the pivot point for all races, including humans. Three different human armies desired to lay claim to the stone Temple and the power that dwelled within. Innumerable years of violence passed with countless deaths of both humans and Lyukians. When the Temple was nearly destroyed, the humans and Lyukians struck a bargain. The Lyukians would take their leave of the Continent and the humans would uphold the Lyukian tradition of alliance by

becoming one people and restoring the Temple. The last condition of the truce was not so simple. The chosen leader of the humans would wed one of the Lyukians' finest warriors and they would unite all who wished to remain in those lands.

"The strongest human warlord gave his daughter upon the agreement of the others, and the Lyukians chose a suitable young Mawyl who was a great warrior, but who was also wise and kind. The humans deigned to call him King Lucan, after his people, and his heirs were the only ones permitted to sit on the throne.

"Although the humans made the bargain based upon the power said to radiate through the walls of the Temple, now the palace of the Lucan bloodline, with every generation that passed the power grew weaker and finally disappeared, much like those who had built it."

Sars closed the book with a dull snap. I pulled back from the table and stared up at him. Our people were that ancient?

15
Missing

"WYNNA, WAKE UP!" I grasped her shoulder and shook her frantically.

"Huh? Wha-what's wrong?" she grumbled, pushing up on her elbows.

"I remember!"

"Remember what?" she yawned.

"I remember where I've seen that language before. The one in the little books," I said excitedly.

Wynna sat all the way up and stared at me. "I guess we should get started then." She swung out from under her blanket and slipped a tunic over her head.

The main room was nearly black as pitch and the sky above the crystal dome was barely brightened by the sun's first light. Wynna lit a lantern and shoved papers aside to place it in the center of our table. We threw ourselves into the complicated translations, searching and searching for combinations of letters that would solve the puzzle. We worked right through breakfast and up to midday. The cook personally brought us food and watched us eat it.

"I'm not going to have any more good food going cold and coming back to my kitchen," she warned us.

Wynna and I laughed. We were grateful for her sentiment, but also felt some irritation. Not just for the intrusion, but also our inability to complete the translation key.

After the cook left, Wynna went right back to work, but my

determination was all but spent. I flopped down with a sigh on the surface of the table, scattering a few papers and one of the little books. I yelped and rubbed at the zing of energy that shot into my elbow. The papers fluttered down around me, and the book tumbled across the floor a little way, the front cover falling open.

I made a frustrated sound and stood to collect the mess I had made, Wynna's gaze following me the whole time. I shoved a hand into one leather glove and scooped up the book. The scribble on the inside cover of the tiny torturous thing caught my eye as I turned back towards the table. At that moment the answer occurred to me.

"Wynna, I'm an idiot," I said, feeling rather limp as I tossed the book onto the table. I yanked the glove off and grabbed a chunk of charcoal. I wrote down the sentence on a new piece of parchment and slid the partial key a little closer.

"What are you talking about?" Wynna creased her forehead at me.

"The answers were right in front of us the whole time. I'm an idiot for not noticing it sooner," I grumbled. My hand flew over the parchment as I put the pieces of the translation together. Wynna's chair scraped as she got up from her seat and moved around the table to peer over my shoulder.

Lyukian blaad ahri zhel nat hevi esiz.

Lyukian blood ahri shall not have access.

Lyukian blood here shall not have access.

"That's it: 'he' in our modern language is 'ah' in the old tongue," I said, recording it on the key page.

"There are more though," Wynna added.

"I don't think there are as many as we may have originally thought.

Try translating a few sentences and I'll see if I can find the next combination."

Wynna went back to her seat across the table and bent over one of the other tomes. While she began scribbling, I looked over the documents in front of me, searching for something that appeared more complicated than it might actually be.

"From what I can tell, that must have been the final piece because everything I'm reading translates fully," Wynna said after a time.

"I still feel like there's one more part missing..." I replied absently.

Across the table, Wynna gently closed the mysterious little book she was using and shoved it towards the center of the table. The words printed on its cover caught my attention and I imitated her, closing the book that still rested on the wood in front of me with a gloved hand. I read over its title and asked, "Wynna, what does 'Tahm' mean?"

She stared at me for a moment and then slid the other book back towards her, peering down at its cover. "The only word that would fit with the rest of the title is 'tome.' The last part of the key must be 'me' in our language was 'hm' in the old language."

I slumped back in my chair. That had to be the last one. We had completed the translation key. Next came deciphering the information the three books contained. Why had it taken so long to figure out something so simple though?

A fuzzy, sluggish part in the back of my mind cleared. The impression of annoyance brushed against my consciousness. I would always be able to recognize that twisted essence. Rafas had been tampering with my reasoning skills for months on end. He had been trying to prevent me from figuring out how to read those books. Rafa had found me, despite all my hope of remaining lost to him. An incurable hatred boiled in my gut, turning to a rage that I would save for the next time we met.

"Nika, are you alright?" Wynna's concern damped down the flame inside me.

"I was wondering what purpose the sentence on the inside of each of these books serves," I said, not totally a lie.

"That is a good question. It refers to 'Lyukian blood,' whatever that means."

"I am Lyukian."

"What? But you're human." Wynna's voice rose with confusion and disbelief.

"Wynna, you've seen bits of what I can become, and you still think I'm just human?" I said calmly. "I'm sorry, but if you thought I was simply the victim of some curse, then you were wrong. I remember enough of my past to know I'm not cursed and I'm not human."

Wynna took a deep breath and slowly let it out. "I suppose you're right. Humans do not have the capability of manipulating magic strong enough to curse people. Besides, magic has all but disappeared from the world."

"It can't have completely disappeared or faded away. I believe it's just gone dormant," I told her and instantly kicked myself.

"How do you know that?" she asked with wide eyes.

"I...don't know. My instincts just tell me that it can't simply be *gone*."

Wynna was silent for a few minutes and I could see the wheels turning in her head. "With that in mind, whenever you try to touch the books with your bare hands pain laces up your arms. That simple sentence must be anchoring an enchantment to the books that is meant to prevent Lyukians from accessing the information inside."

"Why would someone want to keep Lyukians from reading the books though?"

"Perhaps the contents were meant to give humans the advantage and the enchantment intended to prevent Lyukians from destroying the books... I don't know anything about Lyukians, but what I have seen from you tells me they are a powerful species. Humans tend to crave dominance over others, and the Lyukians probably posed as a formidable adversary at one point."

"That is likely, but the magic on the books must be extremely old and greatly depleted if I am able to avoid it by just wearing gloves." I held up one of the leather gloves.

"Indeed... It is a wonder the books have survived this long if the enchantment has faded so much," Wynna pondered, staring straight through me. Her eyes flickered towards the curtained off section of the library briefly before she sat up straight and said, "I think it's about time we learned something from these pests."

I burst into laughter and she sat smiling broadly at me across the table. The tiny tomes certainly were pesky and had caused both of us innumerable headaches for months.

After about an hour of translating sentence for sentence and writing down our conclusions, we both had pretty well memorized the key for the old language. Having a shortcut for learning the old language certainly made the final part of our job much easier, even though finding the shortcut had been a time-consuming hassle to say the least.

Eventually we were able to lean back in our chairs and simply read the text in the tomes, only deciphering a few words on paper once every few pages. We did write down the most interesting information and had a wonderful time pouring over the tiny, detailed images sketched in the books. The sketches depicted the physical aspects of Lyukians that differed from those of humans.

The Kylth were wolf people who had great physical strength and size, even when they hid their Lyukian form. When they revealed themselves, they resembled men or women covered in fur ranging in color from black to brown to almost white. In essence, they looked like crosses between humans and wolves.

Mawyl appeared similar to eagles with large wings and feathers covering their bodies in varying shades of brown. The text reported that their wings were normally tipped with white or gray, depending on age. The younger Mawyl had darker wing tips compared to those of older members of their race. They were also reported to be only male and could only bear male children.

The last race we read about sent sparks throughout my body. The Lykke race was very similar to the Kylth, but slender in stature and had the appearance of a wild feline, usually of tawny coloring. They tended to be relatively tall, but not extremely strong like the Kylth. Supposedly, the Kylth were a warrior race and the Lykke a race of assassins. Of course, in times other than war those duties would be much different.

It appeared that all three races intermarried regularly, but there was mention of something that Wynna and I concluded was a fourth race called Iryl, which complicated the reproduction of the species. Although there was nothing that said how they complicated it. There was very little mention of the Iryl in any of the books, so we suspected that they were extremely rare.

"Wynna, since we have one tome for each race here, shouldn't there be another one for the Iryl somewhere?" I asked her, drawing my eyebrows together.

I put down my chunk of charcoal and shut the tome I had been reading. I had no idea how long we had been sitting there, but the sun had set many hours before and my rear end had no shortage of complaints.

"Hmm...in theory that would be true, but since there was so little mention of them perhaps the author never acquired enough information to put it into a binding." Wynna stood, dramatically clutching at her backside and shuffled towards our quarters. "Either way, I'm going to bed before my back snaps."

I followed her slowly, my head wrapped in layers of new information. None of which particularly helped my situation, though I did have a source of information about Rafas.

"Either way, there is still so much *missing*," I mumbled as I slipped into bed. Wynna's familiar snores drifted through our little stone room as I struggled to fall asleep.

Light burst across my vision. I squeezed my eyes tightly shut again. The soft cushion of a bed and pillows pressed into me. A breath hitched in my throat as my fingertips grazed every individual fiber of the weave in the sheets. There was the murmur of voices talking somewhere across the manor. If I listened very carefully, I could almost make out the words...

The voices turned into the sound of footsteps pounding in my head.

All the noises around me came crashing into my mind: Bena chopping vegetables and boiling water in the kitchen, birds chirping and squirrels chattering outside, the frogs by the small pool in the garden croaking and splooshing into the water. All the sounds were so vivid that the images of them crowded behind my closed eyes.

And the constant thumping, pounding of those footsteps growing louder and louder, nearly drowning out everything else. My hands flew to my ears as a blood-curdling scream tore itself from my lips. I wanted it all to stop. *If I screamed loud enough maybe I could drown everything out.*

Through the pain and chaos, I barely caught the sound of my own name. I didn't understand it at first, but it kept repeating over and over again until it too was threatening to shatter what little sanity was left inside me.

I gasped for air and my eyes flew open in desperation. I searched for something to tether me to reality, only to be blinded by the light pouring in through the windows and the agonizing vibrancy of all the colors in the room. Every surface was pulsing and vibrating. I could see *the ridges and crevasses of the texture of the wood walls and each stitch in the tapestries.*

Nothing was familiar any more. Tears welled in my eyes, obscuring the foreign world for a moment before coursing down my cheeks and dripping onto my chest. A face filled my sight, blurred by my tears.

"Nika, I need you to trust me and take slow, deep breaths." Lord Rafas's voice sounded far away, like he was talking through water.

I stared at him, words no longer making sense to me. The air moved against my body as he lifted his hands toward my face. I felt the crackle of energy just before his skin touched mine. The contact sent a shiver of ice through my veins, silencing the hurricane inside my mind and banishing all abnormal sights with a dizzying effect. I fell into a dazed state of no conscious thought for what seemed like hours on end, but that concerned face was always within my vision.

I only managed to come back to myself when a warm liquid was poured into my mouth. I jerked forward, sputtering and wheezing. A sigh of relief alerted me to the presence of others. Lord Rafas sat next to me on the bed and Bena stood nearby clutching a steaming mug to her breast. Lord Rafas leaned back as though he was going to let his hands drop from where they clutched the sides of my head.

"No, don't let go!" I squealed, clamping my own hands over his and squeezing them tighter against my temples.

"It's alright. I've dampened down your senses again. They won't come back like that until you want them to," he said, holding my frantic gaze.

"Why in the Kingdom would I ever want them back?"

"They will be very useful once you know how to use them," he replied, slipping his hands out from under mine.

I whimpered and winced as he let go, braced for the explosion that didn't come.

"Drink this, it will help you recover." Bena handed him the mug and he held it out to me.

I took the cup from him and almost dropped it when I saw tiny yellow feathers covering the backs of my hands and arms. I reached up and touched my cheek. The feathers stopped just below my cheekbones and under my chin. I felt my hairline to find that the fine strands of hair that were so familiar had been replaced by feathers that became longer and longer the farther back I felt. They weren't stiff and coarse, but almost as flexible as hair *and even softer.*

"Wh-what is this?" I said quietly, examining my hands again.

"It will go away in a day or so, but you'll get a fever. The simple explanation is that you are not human." He scraped stray strands of hair back out of his face and took a deep breath.

"How is that possible? My father is human. I never knew my mother, but he would never marry anyone who wasn't human. There aren't even any non-human people in the known world," I sputtered, barely keeping my shock in check.

"Most likely your father didn't know what your mother was until after you were born."

"He did say I was a monster, just like my mother…"

"You are not a monster. I promise you that," Lord Rafas said, taking my hands and gripping them firmly. "In ancient times, a species of people just like you ruled the Continent. They still exist in the farthest reaches, but no longer show themselves."

"How do you know?" I squeaked.

"I was born among them."

16
News

RAFAS'S WORDS ECHOED through my head as I woke. The Lyukians hadn't left the Continent after all. They were hiding and Rafas knew where to find them.

"Nika, are you awake?" Wynna said softly across the room.

"I'm awake." I rolled onto my side and smiled at her, blinking my bleary eyes.

"Did you have another dream last night?" she asked cautiously.

"I didn't wake you, did I?"

"It's alright, I don't mind. You were quite uncomfortable though." There were questions in Wynna's eyes that she was too polite to ask.

After a moment I told her, "I remembered learning that the Lyukians are still here somewhere on the Continent."

Wynna's jaw dropped and then she was crouched on the floor in front of me. I had never seen her get out of bed that fast, even for the king. She was clutching the edge of my blanket in both fists. There was a wild hope in her eyes that astonished me.

"Are you serious? You're not just telling me that, right?" Wynna sounded like a child, eager and full of wonder. "If we could ever find them or if they decided to come back, there would be so much they could teach us."

I opened my mouth to reply.

"Wynna!" Her name boomed through the library, ricocheting off the stone walls and vibrating our insides.

"Uh oh, this can't be good." All the cheerfulness vanished from

Wynna's face in an instant.

Her hands left my blanket like they would a prized possession as she stood. She hastily got dressed and gave me very brief instructions to finish putting away the stack of manuscripts that had just been returned from one of the manors before reading any more from the Lyukian tomes. She was gone before I could even finish pulling my tunic over my head.

With a sigh, I went out into the main library where our breakfast sat on one of the tables, completely untouched. I hoped the king would have something for Wynna to eat. Then again, if the whole palace heard Prentivus calling her, which I wouldn't doubt, perhaps the kitchens had already sent food to the king's offices.

The manuscripts were piled on the same table, keeping the food company like they were old friends. When I say piled, I really mean heaped. I didn't want to know how long it had taken to read all those manuscripts. Plus, there was the issue of getting the unbound pages mixed up. The thought made me cringe. Plunking down in a chair nearby, I regarded the stack with steaming disdain and chewed my breakfast slowly, postponing the moment when I would have to start replacing the manuscripts on their rightful shelves.

The manuscript project, just as I had suspected, took much longer than I would have liked. It was unquestionably the most difficult task Wynna had ever given me. The manuscripts were all based on different topics and some were in foreign languages that I couldn't even begin to understand. I had to go from one side of the library to the other and back again numerous times. Not to mention teetering on the tops of ladders.

Just before noon, I spread myself on the floor with leather gloves on hand and opened the Lykke tome. Wynna and I had discerned that the most unique information about each race was located towards the back of the books. I flipped toward the back half of the book that might reveal valuable information about Rafas and went to work.

It couldn't have taken more than a couple hours before I had combed through the entire section that was most likely to yield results. All I had found was one sentence that basically read, "Inherently bent on self-improvement and entirely too aware of their own flaws."

"What is that supposed mean? Taunt them and they'll lose their minds?" I wondered out loud, tossing the tome back onto the table.

I rolled onto my back and gazed up through the glass ceiling to the drifting clouds above. They were darker than usual, and a gust of wind filled with red leaves swept by overhead. Summer was certainly over and soon autumn would be too.

"Hello? Nika, are you in here?" A familiar voice accompanied the scrape of the door.

I sat up quickly, peering over the edge of a table towards the hall. I was surprised to see Eith carrying a tray of food. I noticed there was a confidence in her posture that I had never seen before and the lines around her mouth were deeper, as though she had been smiling more frequently.

"Nika, what in the Kingdom are you doing on the floor?" A smile broke out across her face and I found myself smiling too.

I jumped up and patted any dust off of my clothes. "I just got tired of sitting in a chair."

Eith started laughing. *Laughing.* I had heard her laugh before, but this was different. Before it had been only the impression of laughter, this time her heart laughed with her. She reminded me of Malvin.

"What are those gloves for?"

"These? Oh, there are some books and papers that we can't touch with our bare hands, so we use these to take care of them," I explained.

"Preserving the books of this library is an important job." She nodded, moving aside some loose papers and setting the tray on the table nearest the door. I almost told her that I was referring to the preservation of my hands but decided against it.

"What are you doing here? Doesn't Rani need you as an accomplice for one of her pranks?" I asked, changing the subject. We sat down at the table where she had placed the tray.

"Rani is spending the afternoon with the king, so I thought we could have lunch and spend some time together like we used to."

"Wynna is with the king though," I said, puzzled.

"I know, the king encourages his children to participate in all Kingdom affairs, no matter how unsavory," she explained briefly. "In fact, right now all of them are with the king. Well, except for Amr."

"Why isn't he there?"

"Amr has far more important business to attend to than to sit in on his father's," Eith replied, rolling her eyes. "He's probably flirting with one of the young kitchen maids or in the stables with the horses, now that they've released him from the hospital."

We giggled at the young prince's expense before I asked, "How is he feeling?"

"Amr is perfectly fine, other than itching to get his arm out of its sling. He is one of those few people who are in the exact same mood no matter what."

"I know someone else like that," I said, winking at her.

"Me? No, I'm not like that. I change all the time," she laughed.

"You certainly seem much different today compared to the day we went to the stables."

"Oh, well, I am much happier," Eith said quietly, her expression becoming sober. "I wanted to thank you for that day."

"You too? I've already been thanked by the king and Amr and…"

"Not for that. I want to thank you for not giving up on me when I had given up on myself." A blush rose on her cheeks. "You made me face my past by encouraging me to reunite with Vernier, and now I can think of the future."

"I wouldn't have called it 'encouraging.' It was more like you had no other option," I pointed out.

"Well, I am thankful no matter what it is you want to call it," she said with a smile.

"I may not have ever had more than a handful of friends in my entire life, but I do know that's what they're for," I replied.

We grinned at each other and ate our food in silence until I leaned one elbow on the edge of the table and said, "How is Vernier, and the rest of the palace, since I don't get out nearly as much as you do?"

"You and Wynna certainly do take your work seriously." Eith lowered her voice as though Wynna might be hiding behind one of the standing bookshelves. "I've heard from just about everyone that the only time Wynna is ever seen outside the library is when her arms are full of books and scrolls and she's climbing the stairs to the king's chambers."

I burst out laughing. She shushed me, waving her hands and glancing from side to side, which made me laugh even harder.

"Anyway, you didn't want to hear about your boss. Vernier…basically started sobbing as soon as we were out of sight at the stables, but in a tough big brother kind of way. I was in a state of total shock until he started talking about how he had searched for mother and me for years. He said that even when he rode all the way to the Moving Mountains, he never gave up hope that he would see us again one day." A single tear sparkled as it ran down Eith's cheek and fell onto the back of her hand where she had folded them in her lap.

"Did he say what the mountains were like?" I said softly, trying to steer her mind away from where I knew it was going.

She took a deep breath and continued. "They were covered in the finest snow he had ever seen and glittered from top to bottom. He rode from one end of them to the other and back, searching for a way through. Every crevasse and tunnel came to a dead end and when he looked for them again, they were gone. Likewise, new ones had appeared in places where there had been none before. He said there was an eerie feeling about them, as though there was always someone watching from above."

"Hmm… I suppose that would explain why they are called the Moving Mountains," I murmured.

"Nika," Eith suddenly perked up, "another thing that is peculiar is that High Prince Ecco has spent every moment with Rani and I since the two of you went for that walk. He has been unusually serious and uncomfortable lately and only made any sort of comment when you were mentioned."

"I'm sure they weren't kind comments," I grumbled, leaning back in my chair and crossing my arms over my chest. "I don't know why I would care if he was 'unusually serious and uncomfortable' as you say,"

"Oh, stop it," Eith scolded.

"What?"

"I know you like him, even if you won't admit it to yourself. Besides, you don't look very attractive when you make that face."

I stared at her, my mouth falling open, and then I just started laughing. I threw my head back and laughed to the domed ceiling. When I could catch my breath, I saw through watering eyes that Eith was glaring at me.

"You know, I've missed our talks immensely," I grinned at her.

Someone cleared their throat from the doorway, startling Eith and I. Of course, it was Ecco sneaking up on us again. Why was it that every time I saw him my skin started prickling?

"What do you want?" I snapped at him.

Eith's jaw dropped. Apparently, she was too appalled by my behavior to scold me.

"I would like to know about this rumor that has come to my attention about how you have a crush on me," he replied coolly, not moving a muscle.

"Don't try and put it all on her," Eith butted in.

I praised her silently in my head.

"Everyone can see that you're practically head over heels for her but can't get out of your own head long enough to notice," she added with a glint in her eye.

I was about to chastise her for making the situation worse, but then I noticed the ashen look on Ecco's face and had to turn a bark of laughter into a snort. In the end, I was glad Eith was always on my side, no matter what she said in the meantime.

Ecco stood there like marble for so long that I leaned over the table and whispered to Eith, "I think you broke him."

"I heard that," he barked at us, "and I happen to know that Miss Liffei has a romance in the works herself."

"Is that true, Eith?" I turned to her.

"I won't deny it, and I was going to tell you, but this imbecile had to interrupt us," she fumed.

I was afraid that steam might start coming out of her ears.

"It's not my fault you left the door open," Ecco countered, motioning over his shoulder. Sure enough, Eith had neglected to shut the library door behind her.

"Wait a minute, he didn't deny anything either," I said over them, waving my hands in the air.

"You're right, he didn't." Eith started scanning him up and down like a prized animal on display.

He gave us a despising look and growled, "Ranalani requested that I tell you she would like you to meet her in her rooms. That is the *only* reason I came here."

He turned on his heel and stormed back out of the library. I listened as his footsteps receded down the hallway towards End Wing. Wynna appeared barely a moment later with an armful of scrolls and an appalled look on her face.

"What's got him in such a sour mood?" she inquired, glancing from me to Eith and back again.

"I believe that would be Nika's fault, as usual," Eith said smoothly.

"Excuse me? It was you who brought up a terribly uncomfortable topic," I argued.

Eith stood and sauntered to the door, her dark braid swishing behind her like the tail of a pleased cat. She paused in the doorway, gripping the edge of the door, and peered at me.

"I suppose there must be some truth to it then, if it's uncomfortable for you," she teased and stepped outside, pulling the door with her.

I stood quickly, nearly knocking my chair over, and called after her, "What about that romance of yours?"

Her voice drifted in through the remaining crack, saying something like, "Maybe another time," and I just slumped back down in my abused seat.

"Looks like you had a busy afternoon." Wynna approached cautiously and dumped her armload on a nearby table.

"I would rather not talk about it," I mumbled towards the ceiling.

Wynna took Eith's place at the table and studied me for a moment. "Come on, you know I'm a sucker for romantic gossip."

"It's nothing new. You and I have already had this conversation," I groaned, resting my arms on the table. Wynna gave me such an interested and patient look that I finally sighed and told her about the interaction between Ecco, Eith and I.

She just nodded and said, "Oh, that again."

I glared daggers at her, but she smiled briefly and placed her hand on my arm from across the table.

"Do not be upset with Eith. I believe she was trying to bring Ecco out more than irritate you. It appears that she at least succeeded in rattling him, and who knows, maybe you'll even thank her one day."

I made a sound expressing that I didn't think that would ever happen. Then I changed the subject by telling Wynna that I had put all the manuscripts away but hadn't found anything more useful about the Lyukians.

"That's alright, the basic information about them is already more than enough." Wynna and leaned her head against the back of the chair and closed her eyes.

"Was it another rough day with the king?" I ventured, not expecting any actual facts from her.

"You could say that," she said, pressing the heels of her hands against her eye sockets.

I nodded, expecting that to be the end of the conversation. I wrapped my fingers around the ends of the food tray and took it to the door.

"The king has received news of Lord Rafas's activities."

The tray nearly fell out of my hands as I placed it next to the door. If the king was in contact with him, there was nothing stopping Rafas from claiming me as a runaway. He could even provide documents of sale from my father, which would force the king to send me right back into his hands. I returned to my chair, my footsteps measured as I tried to keep my legs from buckling underneath me.

"The king has been watching Lord Rafas since his break in communication with the capital," Wynna continued.

I took a deep breath and slowly let it out, calming my nerves. I was still safe from him, for now.

"The reports that the scouts brought back were quite disturbing. It appears that Lord Rafas is using both North and East Manor as housing for mercenaries."

"Are you serious?" My jaw went slack as a shiver crept over my body.

"The king is in total disarray. It looks as though Lord Rafas is planning some sort of attack. The grounds surrounding the manors are full of mercenary campsites, and they use the main courtyards for sparring." Wynna dropped her head into her hands and her shoulders drooped. "I'm afraid all my knowledge and wisdom can't help the king very much this time."

"I'm sure just your presence eases the king's mind to some extent. There must be something for you to do, otherwise he wouldn't always be asking for you." I reached across the table and placed a hand on her shoulder.

"I suppose you're right. I just have to keep trying." She slowly lifted herself from the table. I hadn't realized that the sky had turned orange above us until a yawn snuck up on me. Wynna circled the shelves, dousing the lanterns. When the lights were out, we filed into our room like sleepwalkers and flopped on our mattresses.

"Maybe tomorrow will be a more promising day," Wynna said.

The canopy of fabric above me looked like water frozen in mid-ripple. Every day I stared at that canopy for hours and never knew why it seemed so soothing. The folds and waves encompassed my mind and made me forget about the pain and fear. I couldn't remember why I was so afraid, but I knew that the reason would return, and I would know it then.

A scraping on the floor barely broke through my consciousness, and it didn't occur to me that someone had entered the room until they were shaking me. The face was familiar and kind, though there was something strange and frantic about it.

"You must get up!" the woman whispered harshly. She grabbed my arms and yanked me up off the pillows and then snatched a cup from the bedside table. There was always a cup there, but I never knew if it was always the same one or not. The woman shoved it in my face and placed a hand behind my head saying, "Drink!"

I tried to grip the cup with one hand, but I couldn't get my fingers to close. I stared at the cup, watching my fingers refuse to wrap around it. I whimpered and looked at the woman apologetically. She just shook her head and brought the cup to my lips, tilting my head back and forcing me to drink until there was no liquid left. I came up sputtering.

"This has gone on long enough," she muttered. I assumed she was talking to herself because I had no idea what she was referring to.

I regained my breath and wiped the liquid off my face. She grabbed one of my arms again and towed me to the door, pausing to peer down the hallway in both directions. My head started spinning and my stomach tried to leap up my throat. I didn't know when I had eaten anything last and that liquid seemed to be boiling my intestines.

I gasped and moaned when the woman pulled me into the hallway and started walking with a very clipped pace. She shushed me and continued down a curved flight of stairs that probably hadn't been used in years. At the bottom, my knees buckled and hit the stone floor. Heaves wracked my body. The small amount of liquid in my stomach came lurching up and my vision darkened with blotches.

"Thank goodness," the woman breathed. She held my hair away from my face and gripped my shoulders, keeping me from falling flat on my face.

I turned my head and looked up at her, recognition finally parting the misty curtains in my mind.

"Bena?" I said, blinking hard and shaking my head.

"Oh, dear girl." Bena dropped to her knees and wrapped her arms around me. A tear fell from her cheek onto my sleeve, but a moment later she was back on her feet. She lifted me from the floor, looping her arm around my waist.

I opened my mouth to ask why we were sneaking through the manor when she whispered in my ear, "I know you must have many questions, and I probably don't have the answers for all of them. First off, we must be very quiet and move quickly. Lord Rafas believes I am in the kitchen cleaning up from supper. I overheard him and Tenley discussing 'the final step' earlier today. I do not know that that means, but I do know it has everything to do with you."

She stopped in the middle of a cobweb strewn corridor, listening very carefully. After many minutes she breathed, "That sneaky little bastard could be lurking anywhere."

I knew she was referring to Tenley and nodded in agreement. We continued to the end of the hall where a thick door with a giant iron lock blocked our way. Dropping her arm from my waist, Bena took a ring of keys from under the folds of her skirts. She began testing all of the largest keys in the lock on the door. As she worked, she started talking quietly again. I leaned in close to hear what she was telling me.

"I would not be surprised if Lord Rafas is planning on marrying you tonight and keeping you as a pet to do his bidding. It is the middle of spring and the two of you had planned on being married months ago." The sadness in her voice was clearly audible and my gut twisted at what she had said. "He

has been having me study the properties of Miasma Root to find different uses for it. I found a way to use the leaves of the plant to temporarily counteract the effects of the root, but my Lord has been searching for a way to use the root to bend one's mind to his will instead of just clouding judgment and memory."

"What is Miasma Root?" I asked her just as quietly.

"There is no time to tell you everything. Just know that you must get away from here and remain as far away from him as possible. You already know he will use you to gain more power at any cost, though you may not remember it."

The lock finally yielded with a grating clack and I helped her shove the door open. Cool night air poured into the hallway. I closed my eyes and took a long, deep breath.

Bena touched my face briefly and then took my left hand in hers. As she gently removed the silver band from my ring finger she said, "You won't need this anymore."

"What about you? Won't he kill you if he finds out you helped me escape?" I said, grasping her hand firmly between both of my own.

"No, he needs me too much. At the very least he might imprison me in the kitchen, which wouldn't be too much different," she tried to smile but only succeeded in forming a grimace. "You must go quickly. The tonic I gave you will wear off in a few hours and the Miasma will return, though not as strongly. Before that time comes, you must fly as far from this place as you can. Fly days and nights if you must."

She shoved me out the door and started to inch it closed behind me. I was outside the manor walls. The edge of the forest was only a few meters away. The night sky was clear and full of sparkling lights. I looked back towards the manor and whispered to the shrinking crack in the doorway, "Thank you."

I turned to face what was ahead with as much courage as I could muster. Calling up my wings was the hardest part. All I remembered from using them was pain and terror, but that could have just been Rafas's doing. I wished I could remember farther back than just a couple months.

I clenched my teeth against the scream that came with the change and took long, deep breaths afterward. The wind lifted my feathered hair from my shoulders as though it was urging me to join it in the sky.

I leaped from the ground, spreading my wings. They lifted me up over the treetops, where I glided on the warm spring wind. A cry rang out through the night. It sounded like the scream of an enraged feline. The feathers along my spine stood on end and I let the instinct to flee engulf me.

17
Exposed

I COULD BARELY OPEN my eyes, let alone move. Usually I did well in the morning, but every now and then there was that one morning when I wished it were still midnight. Part of the problem was that I hadn't heard Wynna get up and had slept too late. The rest of the problem was that I had been so busy reliving my liberation from Rafas that even if Wynna had tried to wake me I wouldn't have heard her.

I groaned as I rolled off of my little bed and winced as the muscles in my back pinched. They remembered that exhausting flight too. Terror still clung to the back of my mind, but I shoved it as far down as I could and planted my feet on the ground. I hoped the complaints of the muscles throughout my body would go away after a few minutes.

Staggering through the library, I practically fell into my breakfast, inhaling the wonderful fruit and cooked eggs. The pieces of apple and pear were heavenly, and there were even some grapes. I sat back and just rolled them around in my mouth for a few minutes, savoring the flavor. Above me, the sky was dark with clouds heavy with impending rain.

I was surprised to see that Wynna hadn't left me a stack of books or scrolls to organize. Walking around the library, I spent quite a while straightening the books on all the shelves that I could reach. I paused in front of the tapestry when I reached its false shelves. I took in the exquisite detail of each book and scroll and the embroidered woodwork in between them. I ran a hand along its surface as I walked, knowing the books weren't real but half expecting to feel their individual spines.

I moved on to the bookcases that stood free of the walls. The shelves held mostly scrolls and manuscripts, which weren't quite as easy to organize as bound books. As long as they were grouped the right way, I left them alone. Rounding a corner, I accidentally kicked a scroll that had been sticking out from the bottom shelf. It went flying across the aisle and came to a stop after unrolling itself. I cursed and thanked the heavens that Wynna hadn't seen that.

As I started to roll it up again, I noticed it looked familiar. It was a map of North Reach. I hadn't known that North Reach was entirely covered by forest, except for where the snow started in the far north. It showed clearings around all the towns in the Reach. To the northwest I found the mining village where my father lived. Farther north was the village where I had been born, where the snow and the forest met, but I didn't remember anything else about it. Creeks and streams made a web of pathways through the forest, all of them flowing south from the Moving Mountains. They carved deep ravines in the icy landscape and wove between the dense trees farther south.

A soft pattering drifted through the library. I looked up from where I knelt on the floor. The sky outside had turned dark and I squinted to see the blur of rain running over the panes of crystal. Scooping up the map, I tucked it under one arm and lit the lanterns to fend off the darkening atmosphere.

"Nika!" Wynna's voice rang out across the library.

I dropped the last lantern, juggling it to keep it from shattering on the floor and lighting the entire place on fire. Firmly grasping it between my hands, I carefully placed the lantern on its hook. I sucked in a breath and turned toward the back of the library. Wynna leaned over the balcony, gripping the railing.

"I'm here!" I called back to her. "You startled me."

"I'm sorry about that, but I need you to do something for me."

"Alright, what is it?"

"The king has requested a set of maps…I see you already found one of them," she said, gesturing to the map still tucked under my arm. "That's good because I can't leave to come show you where to find them. The rest are in the same section where you got that one, on the shelf directly above it. They are all different maps of North and East Reach."

"You want me to bring *all* of them?" I asked incredulously. There were at least twenty maps in each section and no way could I carry them by myself in one trip.

"Yes, *all* of them. We've sent someone to help you. Bring them up as quickly as you can." She started to turn away and then added, "Oh, and don't be upset about who's coming to help. It wasn't my idea."

Wynna disappeared back into the second floor of the palace. A pang of disappointment tightened in my chest. I wouldn't be able to study that map anymore. I also wished I had known there were so many maps to look at before.

I returned to the bottom shelf where I had so unceremoniously found that first map. I started gathering the rest and moving them to one of the larger tables in the center of the library. Once the section on the bottom shelf was empty, I did the same on the one above it. I took care to keep the scrolls from the different shelves separate. If I didn't Wynna would certainly have something to say about it.

The doors' familiar scrape as they opened sounded through the open air. I took the last of the maps to the table, my arms encircling the tubes of paper. Ecco stood at the opposite end of the table watching me. I paused for a moment, gaining control of the glare that so desperately wanted to plant itself on my face. With a deep breath, I emptied the rolls of parchment on the table.

"Wynna gave me these to make the job easier," he said, holding up a few burlap sacks with long straps. Relief flooded my body and I practically flew to him, grabbing the sacks and holding them up like favorite objects that had been lost for a long time. The prince gave me a strange look and I lowered my arms.

"You try carrying these types of thing all by yourself and you will understand." I glowered at him.

"Whatever you say, Miss Fobess." He sounded almost kind, inclining his head in some sort of acknowledgement.

"What are you playing at?" I propped a fist on my hip, scrutinizing every line and curve of his face.

"I'm not playing at anything," he replied.

I didn't budge.

He shoved his hands in his pockets. "Before I came down here, Wynna basically told me to be nice to you or get skinned alive. Either way, I'm tired of fighting with you."

"Alright, let's get to work then." I tossed one of the bags at him and spun on my heel. He deftly caught it before it hit him in the face. I debated going for a second try.

"That's it? All of a sudden you don't care?" he said, following a little too close behind me.

I started shoving the maps into my bag so that they stood on end. He came up beside me and did the same.

"I still care. I'm just tired of arguing too." I had nothing more to say on the subject, so we stuffed in silence. I only spoke to give instructions so that the geologically different maps were in separate bags.

Prince Ecco hung a bag over each of his shoulders and I slung the third across my back when they were all crammed full. I led the way out of the library and then stopped in the hallway. The prince gave me a questioning look and I rolled my eyes at him.

"You go first, Your Highness. I don't know where we're going."

"Don't call me that, ever," he grumbled over his shoulder as he started down the hall.

"Why shouldn't I?" I asked, putting a skip in my step to catch up to him.

He cast me a sideways glance. I squinted at him until he started fidgeting like a nervous squirrel. He probably only answered to get me to stop.

"I may be called a prince, but I'm not any *higher* than anyone else in this world. We are all born, and we all die," he said shortly, shifting one of the bags.

I stopped and stared at his back as he kept walking. I couldn't believe my ears.

"The first day I met you I never would have expected anything like that to ever come out of your mouth."

He halted and turned halfway, fixing me with his steely silver gaze.

His eyes glinted in a forlorn and yearning way that made my breath hitch.

"I suppose neither of us knows the other as well as we might think," he replied, lowering his eyes to the stone floor.

I studied him for another moment, his unruly dark hair and stooped shoulders. Usually his posture was impeccable, haughty even. Something had changed in him since we first met, or maybe he was just letting his guard down. Maybe I was letting my guard down. After all, any girl would daydream about walking down a hallway with the mysterious and handsome High Prince Ecco. For half a moment, I let myself acknowledge his broad shoulders and strong form. The corners of his mouth turned down slightly and his dark lashes were stark against his cheeks. I was surprised to find myself wanting to take the loneliness out of his features.

He raised his head and looked into my eyes as though he had felt some impression of my thoughts. The loneliness had been replaced by… What? Relief? Hope? The difference in his features took my breath away. I straightened my shoulders, slowly and deliberately closing the distance between us.

"Shall we continue?" I said, clearing my throat as I passed him.

He walked as close to my elbow as the bags of scrolls would allow as we turned into the throne room. No matter how many times I saw it and even though I expected it to be there, the great tree slackened my jaw in awe. It was strange seeing it on a stormy day. The leaves and branches seemed to whisper of untold legends and mysteries that had never been solved. The tree wasn't frightening or looming, it just seemed more willing to give up a few of its secrets, as long as someone was willing to listen.

"Will the tree ever break through the crystal?" I wondered out loud.

"I don't think it will. The highest branches have never touched the roof," Ecco replied, gazing up at the tree like he would an old friend. "It seems as though the ceiling grows as the tree does."

Ecco led me up one of the staircases that curved up over the huge map of the Continent. The staircase itself was a gigantic work of art. Strange and beautiful symbols were etched into the railing, interspersed between the signature lifelike vines and flowers of the palace. The steps themselves looked as though they had just been carved the day before, every ripple and wave within the stone shining bright despite the dim lighting.

The steps were wide enough for two people side by side, but just barely. Ecco's sleeve brushed against the railing every few steps and the satchel of maps that bumped against my hip scraped along the stone wall on my left. The strap was beginning to dig into my shoulder. I shifted under its weight and exhaled sharply, the last step still a long way away.

"Imagine having to use these morning and night," Ecco said roughly in my ear.

I nearly jumped out of my skin, not expecting him to be that close. He just started laughing.

"Did you have to? First you appear out of nowhere all the time, and now you're beginning to have a habit of startling me," I snapped.

Ecco took one look at me and started laughing again. With a groan, I stomped off up the stairs. I focused on the last step, attempting to ignore the sound of the prince's amusement that drifted up behind me.

"Come on, a little joke can't upset you that much," Ecco teased.

The sound of his feet as he jogged up the steps tapped through the throne room. A moment later he gently grasped my elbow. Tingles burst up my arm. I shrugged my shoulder slightly to keep them from spreading any higher.

"Says you," I retorted. My spine stiffened as I fought the urge to move closer to him. I gave him a sidelong look, the corner of my mouth twitching up, and winked. He dropped his hand like I had burned him. A laugh barked up my throat at the expression on his face.

"Well, at least we can laugh at each other's expense, even if we don't ever get along," I told him between giggles.

He made a huffing noise that I took as agreement.

Relief flooded my body like cool water when my foot hit the final step. My heart pounded and the air felt heavy as I sucked it in and out. I didn't think I would ever look forward to making that climb. Beside me, Ecco appeared unphased, bored even. He led me along the railed balcony that looked over the throne room. The balcony curved to run along the opposite side of the second floor. Ecco gestured toward a door placed at the center of the curvature.

"There are my father's rooms. His offices are just behind that door," he said.

"Is the entire second floor basically a terrace?"

"Not quite. The walkway is essentially inside the throne room, but the other rooms are built off of it. The king's quarters are the farthest away from the stairs while the laundry rooms are in the eastern semicircle." He jerked his chin towards the opposite side of the second floor. "The offices and quarters of the advisors are in the western semicircle, as well as guest rooms."

"That doesn't make sense. The first floor of the palace is square, and the throne room is diamond shaped."

"Basically, the second story is a gigantic circle that takes up almost as much space as the entire ground floor. On the north side of the palace, the second story ends with that balcony that looks into the library and the stairs that lead down to the throne room. The rest of the second floor extends over the rest of the palace."

I gave him a blank look. I tried to imagine how the second floor fit together with the rest of the building, but only succeeded in making my brain cringe.

Ecco grinned at me, his amusement palpable. I hadn't realized my jaw had gone slack. I snapped my mouth shut and quickly turned to look where we were walking.

The door to the king's offices opened and half a dozen guards emerged. Each in turn inclined their head to us as they went by. A glint caught my eye. I glanced at the last man in the queue. His movements were stiff, less practiced than the rest of his troupe.

Ecco started talking in my ear about something. I tried to listen but there was an itch in the back of my mind that wouldn't let me focus. I fixed my attention on Ecco, squeezing my eyes shut and then following the movements of his lips. It took all my concentration to make out individual words, but I couldn't put them together into sentences.

Was I getting sick? Had I eaten something bad? I racked my brain for possible explanations.

The final guard passed us. He nodded his head like all the others. When he raised it again, molten gold shone in his eyes. He lunged, wrapping one arm around Ecco's neck and shoving me out of the way with the other.

I stumbled down the walkway, my back cracking against the railing. I gasped in pain and water filled my eyes. I shook my head back and forth, blinking away the tears. My vision cleared, fixing on Ecco's blazing silver gaze. His lips moved as he wrestled with the guard at his back. It looked like he was calling my name, but the pounding and humming in my head drowned out all other sound.

My palm pressed against the searing in my chest, I sucked in air and lifted my other hand toward the struggling men. I took one shaky step forward as Ecco rammed his elbow into the guard's ribs. The guard's mouth curved into a snarl and his arm loosened but no pain showed in his eyes. Ecco pulled away for half a moment. His fingertips just brushed against mine before the guard looped an arm around Ecco's throat again, the elbow under Ecco's chin choking off his air as they backed into the railing. Fear flickered in Ecco's eyes and the breath surged out of me. Then they were gone.

The group of guards rushed the railing their grasping fingers too slow to help their prince. I hopped up onto the rails, swinging both legs over. My heart leapt into my throat as my feet dangled over open air. Below, the guard had released his hold on Ecco, the taint of yellow gone from his eyes and his body once again his own. Ecco was grasping for the branches of the tree but all of them were just out of reach. I heard a shout. One of the guards on the balcony was reaching for me, his eyes wide. I sucked in a sharp breath and slipped from the rail.

Adrenaline shot through my veins, tearing apart my skin and shattering the bones in my shoulders. A scream wrenched itself from my lungs. My vision clouded over with red. The blood pounding in my ears beat away each precious second.

I shrieked in my mind, holding on to consciousness as long as I could. The red started to fade into black, but I focused on falling faster. The floor of the throne room loomed up closer and closer.

I pulsed the air with my wings once, choking on the ripping pain that laced through me. It brought me close enough to wrap my arms around Ecco's waist. The fear in his eyes wasn't nearly as horrifying as the resignation.

My wings fluttered in an attempt to slow our fall, but my body didn't have the strength to carry two people. All of my muscles were slowly fading. Soon I wouldn't have enough strength to keep my grip on him. I rotated just enough so that I would hit the floor first and enveloped Ecco in my wings.

Right on cue, the stones slammed into my back, crushing every fiber in my body. I felt the spider web of fractures that laced themselves along the bones in my wings. I lost control of every part of my body and went limp. My wings shook as they fell to the floor on either side of me and my arms quickly mimicked them.

I sucked in a shuddering breath around the blood that was filling my lungs from punctures created by broken ribs. My head spun. Prince Ecco's face came into view, blurred between the clouds of darkness that were rapidly gathering across my vision. I let the air escape from my body with a rattle. He made it. I could let go.

I never thought that was how I would die.

"What are you saying?" I yanked my hands out from between Sars's. "Have you gone mad?"

I took two steps backwards. The edge of the broad table in the center of his study bumped into my lower back. Morning light flowed in through the tall windows behind his desk. I had looked forward to enjoying the morning with him and learning more about our species. Now I just wanted to get away from the insane words that had come out of his mouth.

"Nika, please!" He reached for me desperately, his eyes pleading.

I slid along the edge of the table away from him. Irritation flooded his features. He lunged forward, grabbing both my shoulders in an unrelenting grip.

"Listen to me! This is our birthright. Our species were the first born on the Continent. It is time the humans gave it back. We should be worshipped like the divine, not hiding out in dark, damp holes like vermin. The greatest throne on the Continent should belong to a Lyukian once again."

"Who would be king? You?" I almost laughed. "I'm sorry, but from what I see here, you are not fit to be a king."

A growl rumbled through him, eyes flashing. Pain burst across the left side of my face. I landed face down on the floor, my palms smacking the wooden planks. I hissed against the sting and the prickle of feathers rose along my skin. I lifted a shaking hand to my blurry eye. Blood came away on my fingertips.

"The Lucan bloodline is weak. They have lost any power they once had. Even the great temple has no power left. They must be eradicated for our people to rise again." Sars's voice drifted through the room with haunting calm. It was his voice, but I no longer recognized the man I thought I knew.

I tossed the screen of my long golden hair out of my face to glare at him over my shoulder. "You would need an army, and no one will follow you. No one."

He took a deep breath and then slowly came towards me. Clamping talons around one arm, he hauled me up from the floor. I could barely touch the boards with my toes. Our bodies were nearly touching, and I had no other choice than to look into his scorching eyes.

"Is that so? Humans are more corrupt and power hungry than even me, my love," he said almost sweetly and then crushed his mouth against mine, using his free hand to keep me from moving my head. He dominated my mouth, his teeth bruising my lips and his tongue choking off my air.

I kicked my feet against the floor, his shins, anything I could reach. I pushed against his chest as hard as I could but still, he didn't yield until he was satisfied. The muscles in my arms screamed from exertion when he finally pulled away. I sucked in a desperate breath, my chest aching.

"My, my, is that how it's going to be on our wedding night?" He tsked at me and shook his head before dropping me to floor.

He turned his back and sauntered across the room. Sars slid into the chair behind the desk, a long arm slung over the armrest as he lounged back into the seat. Using the table as support, I pulled myself up with one hand while the other cradled my mutilated face.

"Make no mistake, you will *be my wife and I* will *get all the power from you I need to complete my goals. If you're a good girl and do as I say I'll make you a queen someday," he said. The most twisted smile I could have ever imagined curled on his face.*

"You can try." I straightened my shoulders and left the office. His burning gaze set my spine on fire as I stepped into the hall. When the door firmly shut behind me, I took off at a dead sprint, stumbling on my skirts as they wrapped around my legs like chains.

18
Voices

THE MEMORY FADED but I still felt the horrible ache in my chest from that day. I reached up with both hands to rub away the pain, but my fingers touched nothing. My eyes flew open. White light obliterated everything, but then started to fade. The faint outline of a room gradually came into focus.

I stood in the back room of the hospital where I had visited Amr just a few days earlier. The room looked exactly the same with its huge curtain and scattered chairs. Everything was so pale compared to how I remembered it.

I thought I heard voices. I blinked a few times and four figures appeared through the white haze. One was hunched in a chair, his head cradled in his hands. Two stood on the far side of the room, their hands fluttering in wild gestures. As my gaze traveled around the room, the last figure was seated on the other side of the bed from where I stood. Their arms were stretched out on the covers, holding someone's hand.

I hoped what I saw wasn't real. I squeezed my eyes shut and opened them again. The image came into focus instead of fading. Wynna braced her elbows against the edge of the bed, her hands clasped around one of mine.

My body was laid on its side, facing away from me. Each golden wing was stained brown with blood and hung limp, trailing on the floor. The feathers covering my back were also darkened where the stones must have broken my skin.

I raised a hand in front of my face but saw nothing, though I could feel the warmth of Wynna's hand against my own.

"How can this be possible?" voices suddenly snapped through the room.

The king was pacing back and forth. Kol stood to the side, trying to be as unobtrusive as possible to his father's marching.

"It doesn't matter. It is possible and now we need to understand what we're dealing with," Kol answered. He sounded as though he hadn't slept in days. The dark circles under his eyes proved it.

"I know what she is and there is nothing to *deal* with because she would never hurt anyone," Wynna said almost angrily. She moved some stray feathers from my hair out of my face as the king stopped pacing and stood by her side.

"Wynna, I know you have become close to her, but there is no way for us to know that for sure. She has been living here for months and at any time could have..."

They are afraid of you. There is no place for you here.

Whispers drifted through my mind. My gut wrenched. I knew that voice.

"Could have what, Father?" Ecco was suddenly standing, fists clenched at his sides. He looked ten times worse than Kol did, and with good reason. I was relieved to see that he appeared unharmed. "Killed someone? Nika saved my life. She saved Amr's life."

"I know, Ecco, but we have to be careful. Nothing like this has ever happened before and no one has ever seen anything like her before. We can't put people in danger by ignoring that." Prentivus faced Ecco, his tone calm despite the tension in his shoulders.

I know where you're hiding.

"There is no way I can just let her go," the king continued.

I am coming to get you back, my love. We will be happy again, I promise.

If Rafas came to the palace, no one would be safe. I had to get away from the capital.

"What is that supposed to mean? Are we going to keep her underneath the guard quarters in that rat-hole of a dungeon?" Ecco moved to the foot of the bed. His eyes flashed like the glint of a blade in the sunlight.

"There is no other choice. We must keep this as quiet as possible. No one is allowed in this room besides Kol and myself."

"What? How can you say that? She sacrificed herself for me and now you're forbidding me from being in the same room with her!" Ecco exploded, stepping up to his father with icy rage burning silver in his eyes.

"Ecco, just go," Kol spoke from the back corner. "There's nothing you can do right now."

Ecco glared at his brother, Kol's simmering blue eyes just as unrelenting as Ecco's. A decade seemed to pass before Ecco stormed out of the room, taking his boiling energy with him.

He won't even try to fight for your freedom. How pathetic.

"Stop it. Leave me alone," I growled.

Ordered around like the dog he is.

Pressure started to build inside my head. Blood was roaring in my ears.

"Wynna, I have to ask you to tell me everything you know. You spent the most time with her here." Prentivus touched Wynna's shoulder gently as he made his way towards the curtain. She just nodded.

"Father," Kol shifted further into the room, "before this quarantine is any more official, Rani and Eith both made me promise to convince you to let them see Miss Fobess."

Since when were Eith and High Prince Kol on a first-name basis?

"Is that so?" The king's face softened. "I suppose a few minutes couldn't hurt."

With a shift of fabric, the king vanished.

Kol mimicked his father and placed a hand on Wynna's shoulder as he passed the bed. He leaned down and whispered something to her that I couldn't make out. The corner of her mouth flickered in an attempt at a sad smile. The prince disappeared around the curtain and then silent tears began to slide down Wynna's cheeks.

Humans are so weak. I don't understand how you can be so fond of them.

"You're wrong." I jerked my head from side to side.

My chest became tight. I wished I could see his face so I could claw it off.

"Dear, dear Nika...I may not be able to change the king's mind, but I will not allow you to rot away in any dungeon," Wynna whispered to me. She held the back of my limp hand to her tear-soaked cheek and then rose carefully from her chair. "I imagine you would be worrying about what might happen to me right now, if you could."

"I am worried about you, Wynna! I'm right here and I don't want anything to happen to you, Eith, or anyone in the Lucan family. I just wish you could hear me," I cried out to her, wanting to reach out for her when she laid my hand back down on the mattress.

Don't bother, my pet. There's no use fretting over such frail creatures.

"You don't know anything," I snapped at Rafas, a snarl catching in my throat.

The curtain rustled, and I turned to see Eith and Rani slipping inside. As Wynna left, she embraced both of them and forced steel into her spine before venturing into the rest of the palace.

The two girls cautiously moved closer to where I lay. When they caught sight of my face, they both seemed to gasp and take in a sigh of relief at the same time, as though they were shocked at what they saw, but also happy that I was actually there.

"I hope you can heal well enough from this. We would miss seeing your pretty face and beautiful smile," Rani said to me. "Thank you for saving my imbecile of a brother."

"Maybe you will remember everything that you lost when you wake up. Then you can finally tell me your story," Eith added. She stepped forward and touched my feathered ankle for a moment, then drew away slowly. "You said that whatever happened we would take it together, so you had better wake up."

I can't wait for you to prove me wrong. I'm sure your argument will be quite delightful.

"You truly are mad." I gasped, Rafas's influence pressing on me.

"Don't worry, Miss Liffei." The king twitched the curtain closed behind him. "The doctors tell me that she is healing at an accelerated rate, an impossible rate actually."

"But she still looks so...broken." Eith choked on the last word.

I moved to her side, glancing down at my own face. I barely

recognized myself. Broken was indeed the appropriate word.

The skin around my eyes were painted purple and brown. My lower lip was swollen and equally as gruesome as the cuts and bruises that peppered the rest of my face and down my neck. Bruises stood out underneath the layer of feathers in dark patches all along my body.

My shoulder was clearly out of place and there was something strange about the placement of my legs. One leg had been splinted from the hip all the way down to my foot, but the bone of my hip was twisted somehow, similar to the look of my shoulder.

See what these humans did to you? They made you mutilate your gorgeous body.

"It was my choice. At least none of them mutilated me themselves." I hissed inwardly and was answered by a growl.

"How can anyone even survive something like this?" Rani asked half to herself, unable to look away.

"In a way she didn't. When the doctors first brought her in from the throne room, her heart was not beating for a long time, but then it would start and stop and finally kept a steady rhythm again. Doctors do not tend to use magic as an explanation, but they believe that her body died while the essence of who she is did not. Something is keeping her alive, whether it is actual magic or the magic of sheer will," King Prentivus finished explaining.

"Do any of them know when she will wake up?" Eith ventured.

"It could be anywhere from a couple weeks to a month. No one has ever seen healing this fast, so no one knows for sure. Plus no one can gauge the actual extent of the damage."

I thought you were the one. Finally, I had found the perfect bride to whom I could bare my soul and would still love me, who would understand my ambitions.

"You never wanted love. You wanted submission and reverence. You wanted a slave!" I spat.

I was wrong about you, but I will get you back. I will create the perfect weapon and you will never defy me again.

"Stay away from me."

You are just as weak as the humans you hold so dear. I will make you powerful and those around you will perish or worship at our feet.

"No!"

I glanced at Eith and Rani who were still speaking with the king. I didn't know what they were saying. Rafas had closed off my mind to everyone else but him.

I am coming and there is nowhere to hide. You won't be able to save anyone this time.

"GO AWAY!"

My mind howled in agony to break the walls he had stealthily been erecting around my consciousness. They tumbled down as I pushed him away with all the strength I had. The pain that wracked my body came flooding in. My physical form jerked and shook. The ringing in my ears overpowered the alarmed voices of Eith and Rani that crashed like waves against my suddenly acute hearing.

My bones were throbbing, each crack and chip screaming for attention. I couldn't breathe, but anything was better than the grip of Rafas's insanity. Pure agony enveloped me. I surrendered to the ache and stab of the physical world. The pale room became as dark as a winter midnight.

~◆~

Blazing, searing fire and rivers of heat devoured my senses with pounding and roaring, climaxing to become the burn of ice and silence. I dreamed of silver and gold, beating wings and slashing claws. Then the cycle reset, every single day.

There was no way to count how many times I shrieked my throat raw and wept myself into dehydration. Time was infinite, holding me hostage in my own body. A few days, a week, a month may have passed but I couldn't even think to care. The instincts of a chained, wounded animal consumed every waking moment as my body forced itself back together from the inside out.

People filtered around me constantly and said the same name over and over. I did not know it was my name. They were all strange to me, even if they had been familiar. The sounds they made were foreign, though my mind knew the words. My body was in total control, consuming all conscious thought for the sake of survival.

When the pain of healing subsided to a slow throb, the chaos of sight and sound and touch replaced it. I heard everything that took place on the palace grounds, perhaps even the city, with agonizing clarity, and this time there was no one to tell my senses to stop. Forced to ride out the storm within my own mind, I managed to teach myself to focus on one thing at a time. First, I chose the texture of the sheets, and then the next day I counted each facet of color in the crystal ceiling.

Every day was an eternity, an eon, but each day I rediscovered the pieces of myself that had shattered when my consciousness returned to my ruined body. As my body healed, so did my mind and my control over my physical form. All the pieces gradually fell into place and the world snapped back into focus.

19
Released

COMPLETE, CONTROLLED SILENCE greeted me when my eyelids fluttered open. The room was filled with the blue-gray of impending dawn, and I felt the sun rising in my very bones. I opened up to the world around me. Some nurses were shuffling back and forth in the main room of the hospital and the faint whistle of birds collecting seeds in the gardens rushed to embrace me. I felt the movement of the air in and out through the heavy curtain and the different scents that rode along with it. I took a deep breath and let it out. The bed was soft underneath me but...the iron that encircled my left wrist and ankle was cold and heavy.

I propped myself up on an elbow. The shackles were connected to freshly driven bolts in the stone floor by a thick loop of chain. I tugged to test their strength.

Metal rang and clacked against metal, sending a cacophony of noise echoing through the room and out into the rest of the hospital. I gasped at the sound, clapping my hands to my ears and collapsing back onto the mattress. My head throbbed, brutally warning me that I still couldn't withstand sudden loud noises.

A yell broke out from the other side of the curtain, shattering what little amount of restraint I had left on my senses. The slam of feet pounded through me and the light in the room became blinding when the curtain was tugged by one of the royal doctors. He said something about the king, but that was all I gathered before my strength fled. I had no choice but to yield to the darkness that was edging its way in.

~◆~

A soft rattle broke the stillness. There was a tug on my foot. My eyes snapped open. I lunged toward the cloaked figure that was hunched over the end of the bed, only to be stopped short when the chain became taut and the figure stumbled back a step. We hung in the silence, regarding each other with bristling panic until they lowered their hood and I saw them as plain as daylight even though the room was almost black.

"Wyn-na," I managed to squeeze out. How long had it been since I had spoken? My throat strained and stung from just that small sound.

"It is me," she breathed. Her shoulders sagged with relief. She clutched a ring of keys in one hand as though her very life depended on them.

"Wh-what a-re you do-ing here?" I wheezed as she went back to work on the shackle around my ankle, trying one key after another.

"I swiped these from the king's office this morning when he came down after you had woken," she whispered, holding up the key ring briefly. "You have to get out of here. I know you're not a criminal, but the king's other advisors will never agree with me and once information about you spreads to Linsdiil and Muirsid, there will be no way for the Kingdom to keep anyone from investigating without a war."

I nodded even though she was too focused on the shackle to notice.

The tight clamp of metal popped apart and sagged around my leg. Wynna silently moved up to the one around my wrist. Not long after, it also went slack. Wynna gently pulled me up into a sitting position. She draped a dark blue cloak around my shoulders and fastened it under my chin, concealing the plain white shift I wore.

"Once we are in the hallway, ask me anything you like, quietly. Until then, we must be silent as dust. If one of the doctors or nurses sees us, it'll be both our heads on the palace gates," she murmured intently.

I nodded again.

She was about to help me stand by slipping an arm behind my back, but hesitated and said, "Um, could you...you know..." She gestured up and down my body.

I hadn't realized I was still in Lyukian form. I took a deep breath and closed my eyes, concentrating on pulling my wings and feathers back under my skin. They retreated slowly at first and then snapped out of sight, leaving me swaying from the effort.

I leaned on Wynna as we sidled through the curtain. Besides a few patients sleeping, there didn't appear to be anyone else in the hospital. Wynna still touched a finger to her lips as a reminder. We crossed the expansive floor, staying as close to one side as we could without knocking over or running into anything. My right leg and hip throbbed with each step. I couldn't quite manage to stand up straight because of the ache that spread along my spine and out across the muscles in my back.

Inch by inch we shuffled silently, clinging to each other. I risked stretching my hearing to try and detect any nearby movement. I gradually broadened my area of interest until it included the corridor outside. I took long, deep breaths to retain control. Footsteps echoed outside, sounding like they were headed toward the doors of the hospital.

Air caught in my lungs as I pulled Wynna towards the doors as quickly as I dared. One of the doors swung inward just as we pressed our backs against the wall behind it. Wynna sucked in a sharp breath and held it as the back of the door nearly touched the tips of our noses.

I peered around the edge of the door. A nurse carrying a tray with both hands shuffled towards one of the occupied beds in the center of the room. I tugged Wynna's sleeve before slipping out from behind the door. We slid along its surface until we could duck around the corner and into the dim corridor. I didn't realize I was holding my breath until it came rushing out of me and I sagged against the wall.

"I'm al-right," I whispered when Wynna's hand squeezed my shoulder in concern. She slid her arm around my waist, and we took up our tiptoe pace again down the huge corridor.

"How long was I asleep?" I rasped in Wynna's ear.

"Tomorrow will be two weeks," she breathed. "The king's advisors have been pushing to have you secured more effectively. The king agreed that two weeks was long enough in the hospital, especially since you were starting to wake up. They wanted to move you before your strength returned."

"The prison beneath the guards' quarters," I muttered.

"How do you know that there are cells down there? Or even a basement to begin with?" She gave me an appalled look.

"I…overheard Ecco arguing with the king." I bit my lip in anticipation of her shock.

"But that was nearly two weeks ago. You had absolutely no consciousness and almost no heartbeat." She struggled to keep her voice level and quiet.

"I don't understand what happened. All I remember is falling and then I was standing outside my own body. It's all a blur of pain, until this morning."

Wynna made a thoughtful sound in response and we rounded the corner past Wash Wing.

"I guess the doctors were right. Some kind of force was keeping you here, even when your body was no longer alive, but no magic can thwart death." Wynna shook her head in disbelief.

I didn't say anything else on the subject. It just left more unanswered questions.

The palace seemed almost too quiet and the stillness set me on edge. I had the lingering feeling that someone was going to jump out and grab us from around a corner. At which point we would both be drug down into the bowels of the palace to never be heard from again

"Wynna, where are all the guards? Don't they patrol the halls at night?" I wheezed.

"Usually they only do their rounds in the throne room and the areas immediately surrounding it, including the second floor. Most of those on duty walk the streets of the capital and guard the gates. Those that are not on duty stay in the barracks," she answered.

We passed the main doors that led out into the West Courtyard and then Wynna led me to another, smaller door. Ducking into the shadows, she came to an abrupt stop and turned me to face her.

"There are guards posted outside all the main doors to the palace and a few that patrol the grounds. We have to be completely silent and tread lightly," she whispered, fixing me with a stern gaze. She pulled me through the little door into the gardens that surrounded Newt Wing.

All the different smells of the gardens mingled with the scents that drifted into the grounds from the city. Damp moss, sweat, and the lingering aromas of various kinds of foods all twined together. I held my breath, searching for something to distract me from the strength of the combined odors. I could just make out the glass dome of Rani's rooms to the north and wondered what would happen when she and Eith found out I was gone.

Wynna didn't give me very much time to contemplate before she was pulling me swiftly along behind her. We crossed a stone path with no more than a light tap of our feet and into a grove of tall ferns. Once the path was out of sight, Wynna shoved me to the ground and flopped down beside me. She lifted a finger to her lips as the soft tread of boots reached my ears. Lost in my own thoughts, I hadn't noticed the approaching guard.

His steps began to fade away. Wynna nudged my shoulder and started to crawl on her elbows and knees through the ferns. I fell in behind her and bit back a gasp at the complaints of my muscles. The bones in my right leg seemed to creak with each movement.

We rose into a crouch at the far edge of the grove. From our position, I could make out the gap in the palace wall where the West Gate would be. I knew Wynna's plan couldn't include crossing the open space of the courtyard and braced myself for the trek around its border through the gardens.

A pathway crossed in front of us that ran the edge of the courtyard. It was rimmed by elegant shrubs that probably bloomed beautifully during the summer and spring. The plants were tall enough that Wynna and I could stoop behind them and not be noticed from the other side of the courtyard.

I clenched the back of Wynna's cloak in my fist for balance and ignored the throbbing in my back as we flanked around towards the gate. Halfway around we ducked behind a couple of giant planters, like the one Rani stole, to avoid another guard. Once we were within an arm's distance from the gate, we had to figure out what to do about the guards posted on the other side.

The crash of breaking glass and screams rang out from down the street, followed by cries for help. Boots rang against stone as one pair of guards took off towards the racket. A few minutes later there was the sound of a struggle and a yell for the other two.

Wynna and I peered through the metal rails of the gate. She raised her eyebrows at me, saying that was a lucky coincidence. The streets were empty of all the life that filled them during the day. Moonlight covered the stones of the lanes and surrounding buildings, painting them with a pale glow.

"I'm afraid that this is where I must leave you," Wynna said softly. She reached forward and pulled the gate open just far enough for someone to slip through.

"What? No! Wynna, they could charge you with treason for this."

"Keep your voice down!" She clapped her hand over my mouth. "No one will know how you got out, trust me. Besides, I'm more use to everyone if I stay here. The king is relying on me with the current state of affairs in the North and East Reaches. Plus, I might be able to buy you more time to get as far away as you can." Releasing me, she put a hand on my shoulder and added, "I'll be fine. Now go."

Wynna nodded toward the gate, but I couldn't budge. I threw my arms around her and held her tight for as long as I dared. Dropping my arms to my sides, I slowly backed toward the gate and squeezed through. I pressed my back to the stone wall on the other side as Wynna swung the gate shut.

I swallowed the lump in my throat and shoved away from the wall. My bare feet padded on the gray stones toward an alley that ran parallel to the main street leading to the western gate out of the city. At each intersection,

I made sure I could still see the main road clearly on the left. I knew the city wall was a long way off, but I had to keep walking even if my feet started bleeding from the stones.

An arm circled my waist as a hand clamped down on my mouth. I was yanked into another alley completely blanketed in shadow. I kicked and elbowed backward. My assailant let go and I stumbled forward.

"That isn't any way to treat a friend," a voice flitted out of the shadows. A moment later they emerged from the darkness of the alley. A hooded cloak concealed their features, but I still recognized them. I only knew of one person who carried themselves that way.

"Daon?" I said breathlessly, shock riding on my voice. "How...what are you doing here?"

"My sister and I still keep in contact, even though that may not seem to be the case," she said simply. Her grin was a bit too knowing for my comfort.

"Is Malvin with you?" I glanced around, expecting the big man to appear at any moment.

"Malvin is sound asleep in the shop right now." Daon chuckled quietly and shook her head at me.

"I don't understand..."

"If Malvin knew what happened to you, he would have an obligation to assist you, but he also has an obligation to the king."

She took a step closer and I noticed the rough bag that was strapped to her back. She shrugged it off onto the ground and crouched to inspect its contents.

"Prentivus and Malvin are decades-old friends. Malvin would be in quite the pickle if he was forced to choose between betraying the king and acting on what he believed to be right. I elected to come to your aid without alerting him to the situation. That is the way Wynna wanted it done as well, understanding my relationship with Malvin."

A pair of black leather boots thumped onto the ground and a pair of dark brown trousers flew at my head. Daon grumbled that I should put them on and ditch the flimsy nightgown. I followed her orders and pulled on the pants. Next, a breast band and a thick long-sleeved shirt were tossed my way.

"Malvin will surely find out what happened in the palace and my part in your release, but I can handle him." She scrutinized me as I refastened the cloak around my shoulders. The last item she pulled out of her pack was a belt and a sheathed dagger. "Hopefully you will never need to use this, but just in case." Daon looped the belt and dagger around my waist and then picked up the bag from where it lay. She held it out to me and said, "There is enough food in here to last you about four days and everything else you might need to survive out there."

I opened my mouth to ask where I might go but decided against it. Instead I said, "Thank you," as I took the pack from her.

Daon made a contemplative sound and narrowed her eyes at me. "It would be easier if you just cut your hair off, but a braid will be fine." She moved around behind me and went to work on the mess of yellow strands. A minute passed and then the feel of her hands in my hair ceased.

"What is it?" I asked.

There was no answer.

"Daon?" I looked over my shoulder to find the alleyway completely empty around me. I ran a hand over the tightly woven braid as the cool of the night settled on the back of my neck.

I slung the pack over a shoulder and started my march towards the western city exit. The sky had begun to take on the gray haze of morning when I reached the gate. I lifted the hood of the cloak over my head before swinging the massive gate open wide enough for me to slip through. I pushed it closed behind me and was greeted by a peculiar look from the only guard who was awake. He gave me a nod and then turned his attention back up the road.

I drew in a slow breath of the crisp morning air and, like the guard, focused on the road that gradually faded into the distance. I urged my legs to move despite the needles that skittered up my bones with every step. My lungs were full of the cool, earthy smell of the stones under my feet. I felt lighter, the sky stretching high above, promising freedom, even though the path ahead would be perilous.

Coming soon...

Clearing the Haze

The Essence Chronicles - Book Two

Don't miss Nika's journey through the wilds of the Kingdom.

Acknowledgements

First, if you are reading this right now, thank you! Thank you for finishing *Breaking the Fog* and I hope you enjoyed Nika's story enough to continue reading about her adventures.

I want to give a huge thanks to Bart Rawlinson's creative writing workshop in the spring of 2014. Everyone gave me the courage and determination to finish the Essence Chronicles and inspired me to create stories centralized around other characters in the Kingdom.

The Essence Chronicles would not be what they are today without the unyielding support of my beta readers and good friends Lindsay and Mark as well as the eagle eyes of my proofreaders, Sharon and my mom. All of your advice and encouragement has been invaluable, and I am eternally grateful.

Last, but not least, I want to extend an epic thank you to my cover designer, Cathy Walker, who knew exactly what to create from the very beginning. Your work is beautiful, and I don't think anyone else could have created a more fitting cover for *Breaking the Fog*.

In 2016, C. C. Mitchell submitted her first ten-minute script to the Mendocino College Festival of New Plays and received the privilege of seeing her play produced along with ten others. *Breaking the Fog* is C. C. Mitchell's first published novel. She has a Master of Arts in English and Creative Writing with a concentration in Fiction and resides in Northern California with her fiancée, chihuahua mutt, a yowling cat, and twenty cows.

Made in the USA
Columbia, SC
17 September 2020

20190310R00143